When

A

Taker

Dreams

Sometime life is not that simple. Love can be complicated.

By

J. A. JACKSON

<u>Acknowledgments</u>

To my best friends' forever Jocelyn, Mary and Lenise. And to my big brother Randy, who is always my June bug. You "all" shine down on me always from heaven. I thank you and I miss you like crazy.

Next up I'd like to give out a big endless gratitude of thanks and appreciation for the wonderful support and editorial guidance of my editor the very knowledgeable Mr. Rossi V. Jackson.

I'd also like to say a special thanks to the incredible man in my life, my husband who believed in my writing and supported my dreams.

Also, to my mother and my father you blew the wind beneath my feet and made me enjoy learning, writing and living this life. God gave me you and you gave me unconditional love and support – Thank you.

Also, a special thanks to my sisters Kay, Shelia and Marie. I am so grateful to you for your support and love. And to my brothers Ray and Eric I thank you also.
For Rossi, Randy, and Daddy & Mommy always….

To my readers and fans, I am forever grateful. Thank you.

He who plots evil...
Will be known as a schemer.
Proverbs 24.8

Chapter 1

The dinner party had started off pretty normal that evening. The guests had arrived, assembled, and collected their cocktails, and now everyone was mingling. Isabella Duvall took her duties, being asked to be a mentor, seriously.

She smiled knowingly. She knew she really wasn't a mentor to the young woman named Cierra. In reality she was grooming Cierra Cantrell to be just like her. Possessed with all of her knowledge and wisdom on how to marry a rich man.

When her older brother, Ryker Granger showed a dark gleam in his eye toward Cierra, she gave him a scolding look of contempt, and quickly steered Cierra out of distance, and into a crowd of people.

At twenty-seven, dark-haired Cierra Cantrell was gorgeous. Growing up in Silicon Valley she had been just your average whiz-kid, with a killer body, and big brown beautiful eyes that sat in a face that was hard to forget.

Quickly, Isabella inserted Cierra into a conversation with two young bachelors that she had invited.

One was Henri Allard. He was an up and coming attorney with Hampstead and Associates. He looked safe with droopy, sleepy eyes.   The other young man was Collin St. Martin, a tall, broad shouldered and handsome professor at the local University. He was the son of Dr. Charleston St. Martin, an affluent owner of a huge local medical supply company. Dr. St. Martin was a very good friend of her mother's.

Isabella gave a sigh of relief. She'd known both of the young men's families and she knew that both of them were perfect and safe for Cierra Cantrell.

All at once Isabella felt a twinge of something. A deep sadness pass through her. *It was Cierra's eyes*, she thought, that had made her agree to watch out for her. It was the grief of knowing that she'd let someone else down once. That woman had had the same haunting brown eyes just like Cierra did.

"Indira Jones forgive me," she mumbled under her breath and felt a cold chill creep down her spine. The moment seemed surreal as she remembered. For an instant she felt a haunting that called out to her from the past. It was the eyes of an invisible phantom who knew she had broken her promise and failed someone in life.

"Hello Isabella! Isabella."

The hand on her arm startled her and awakened her out of her trance.

Isabella sucked in a breath. "Heavens, Dr. Martin, I didn't see you."

"Isabella. Thank you for introducing Collin to Cierra. I like her a lot," Dr. Charleston St. Martin said. "I just hope Collin doesn't bore her to death. You know that Geeky son of mine has no social skills what so ever. By the way, love the dress."

Life goes on, Isabella thought, shaking out her thoughts. "Thank you for the compliment Dr. St. Martin. I'm sure Collin's social skills are fine."

"Well, if Collin strikes out with Cierra I'm going to put his name on every online dating site out there. A father has to do what he has to do."

"Stop worrying Dr. Martin," she assured him. "Remember, I told you I'd give you the number to the matchmaker, Eris Simeon, if things don't work out with Cierra."

He shook his head. "Okay, if you say so Isabella. I'm willing to try anything. But just remember, my son is almost thirty and I want him out of my house!"

The minute Dr. Martin walked out of view Isabella turned around and focused her concentration back on Cierra Cantrell.

So far mentoring Cierra had been easy. Her purpose had been to mold Cierra into her image, ferociously independent, and determined, with a reputation for being business minded in things of work and the heart.

Isabella had changed Cierra for the good in several of those ways except she couldn't seem to shake the girl of her romantic notions or her thinking that a pair of blue jeans and a blouse and sweater was proper attire for everything she did in life. But at least tonight, she had gotten Cierra to compromise and wear the black lace

scallop edged cocktail dress with black patent leather
pumps, she had helped her shop for.

The dress clung to Cierra in all the right places.
Her only regret was that she had not been able to persuade
Cierra to let go of her glasses and wear contacts. But at
least she agreed to wear her gold framed glasses instead of
her usual black plastic framed ones.

Isabella felt a pang of apprehension when she saw
her brother Ryker walk over and join the single people in
their conversation.

She watched as Ryker took over the conversation.
Instantly the two young men scattered like flies. She knew
the maneuvering. Her brother was using his low-down and
dirty hustler, antics to weed out the competition. She'd seen
him use them on unsuspecting, gullible business partners
that got in the way. Her brother Ryker was ruining her
plans.

"Ryker, you scummy street hustling bastard,"
Isabella muttered under her breath, as she stood there a few
more seconds before deciding to close the distance between
them.

Cierra Cantrell wasn't his type. The girl wore geeky
girl glasses and didn't know how to dress herself. Not to
mention she had an innocent streak a mile long.

Before she could reach them a familiar voice told
her, "Damn, is that your brother with another woman? The
fuckin' bastard! I have a good mind to go over there and
make a scene."

Isabella froze on the spot. "Desiree!"

It was Desiree Martin, her brother's ex-girlfriend. She was dressed in a black beaded cocktail dress that looked like it had been painted on.

Isabella was concerned with the drama Desiree could bring. "Desiree, what are you doing here?"

"You knew I was coming," Desiree smiled tilting her nose in the air. "I'm sure our mutual friend Tiffany told you."

Isabella shook her head. Desiree Martin tried to act like she'd been born into money. The woman was a female version of a hustler trying to sleep her way to the top. Still, she was her friend. "Yes Desiree, our mutual friend Tiffany told me you might show up."

Desiree Martin winkled her nose, staring around the room. Giving off an air of sophistication. "At first I wasn't sure I could make it. I so loath these charity fund raiser parties. There is always some low-life trying to start drama."

"Yeah, and normally it's you," Isabella replied with blunt curiosity noticing how she fumbled with her dress. The dress looked two sizes too small. "What's wrong tonight honey your dress too tight?"

"Very funny Isabella. Apparently, my dress isn't doing the job it was supposed to do, attracting your brother, because he hasn't looked up at me one time."

Isabella composed herself and smiled at her candor. "Come off it, Desiree. You're not interested in my brother."

Desiree frowned and sucked in a breath. "Oh…"

"By the way," Isabella quickly interrupted. "I thought I saw you come in earlier on the arm of that basketball player... What's his name? Calvin Harrison," she stated, but didn't wait for a response. "Does Calvin know you have a revolving door with your ex Marquise?"

"Hell, no he doesn't and I would appreciate it if you kept your mouth shut about that subject, Isabella," Desiree snapped. "I thought we were friends."

"I'm sorry I said that," Isabella told her. "We are friends."

"And I'm sorry too for yelling at you Isabella. You know Ryker and I have moved on. It's just that when I saw the way he was looking at that woman he's standing with it made me jealous. I mean I remembered there was a time when Ryker looked at me like that. Damn, he makes me horny just staring at the two of them." She shuddered with her memories and exhaled with a dangerous smile. "I know Ryker must be giving her some good hard..."

"Excuse you," Isabella raised a questioning brow as she glanced in their direction. "Desiree, that girl is my mentee."

"Girl my ass. That is a woman," Desiree laughed. "Oh, don't worry. Ryker and I haven't been an item for a very long time. Anyway, I've got a bad headache tonight, my sinuses are acting up. By the way Isabella, can I ask you to do me a favor?"

"Okay, I'm listening. What do you want?"

"Can you drop by afterwards and check on me? My headache feels bad and I'm going to pop one of my sinus headache pills. You know the ones that can make me do that sleep walking thing," she replied touching her forehead. "Anyway, I'd feel better if you stopped by and checked on me. Here, take my extra key and let yourself in."

Isabella shrugged. "Sure Desiree, but I might not get that way until after two o'clock before I stop by on my way home. You know I have to stay and see this event through to the bitter end," she hesitated. "That reminds me, don't put anything on the stove when you get home. The last time you did you burnt those boiled eggs something awful."

"Okay, fine. I'm not hungry anyway," Desiree replied.

Isabella watched her exit the room.

Just then a tall skinny, blond guy approached. It was Professor Charles Price, the inventor.

"Isabella, where is your hubby Stuart?" Charles asked.

"You know Stuart hates these functions, Charles," Isabella said kissing his cheek in greeting.

"You know, I loathe these parties, just as much as Stuart does. But I make the effort. Especially when you promise me that if I came you would introduce me to that Max Brentwood. You know he sits on the board of directors at Haywood and Associates. They are the most important venture capitalist firm in the Valley."

Isabella nodded grimly letting Charles lead her away.

Across the room Ryker had trouble concentrating as he marveled at Cierra's elegant fingers as they picked the cherry out of her glass and brought it to her lips. He tried to keep his heart in his chest as he watched her.

He watched her sip her drink and lick her lips. The woman was like a sexy goddess, only he could tell that she didn't have a clue that that was what she was doing to him. Instantly he went over.

"Are you having a good time?" Ryker asked, as he approached her.

"Huh," Cierra said, finishing her drink and placing it on a waiter's tray, as he walked past. She breathed out. "Honestly, I don't know what to do with myself, since Henri and Colin walked away. I mean with them I can say the stupidest thing and they laugh."

She scooted in close and said. "Yet, you just stand there staring at me looking and I can't think of a damn thing to say," she exhaled. "Anyway, I figured all that there is left to do now is to stand here and wait for your sister Isabella to introduce me to the next upstanding son of some one," her voice trailed off.

Ryker stood there silently studying her. "Nobody can mistake you for being anything but honest," he laughed.

She looked up. "I sorry I didn't mean that to sound rude."

"No problem your highness, you just said what was on your mind and I can't blame you. Beside I observed you all evening and know you've been stuck under my sister's arm like a string puppet, when you'd rather be off doing something else."

"Oh really, and what do you think I'd rather be doing?" Cierra teased.

Ryker glanced across the room at his sister. There was a slight curve to his lip as he watched Max Brentwood and Isabella. Max placed his hand on Cierra's arm keeping her close to him. Ryker smiled. Thank God good old Max owed him a favor.

"Come on your royal highness let's get out of here. I can tell we both could use some fresh air," Ryker said, taking Cierra by the hand.

Chapter 2

Cierra couldn't believe she had let down her guard and left alone with Ryker.   She was pretty sure it was because he'd called her your royal highness. The way the words rolled off his tongue sent shivers down her spine.

As she got into the passenger side of his flashy Porsche Panamera, she grinned wide leaning into the plush leather seat. She felt like a princess being whisked away. As his flashy car sped away from the front of the hotel she wondered if she'd done the right thing. It wasn't like her to just take off for a drive with anybody.

Ryker didn't know why he'd let his impulse get the best of him. Something about Cierra brought out the protective side in him. He watched her play with a loose strand of her hair.

He gripped the steering wheel tighter. He didn't want her to see how nervous he was. Cierra didn't say a word as he drove.   Out of the corner of his eye he studied her. She wasn't like any of the women he was used to.   She was like an angel who had floated down from heaven with big brown eyes.

Finally, she spoke. "Where are we going? I mean it's not like I don't trust you or anything," she hesitated, her voice was sad. "But we're going for a ride, right?"

At the moment she looked back at him he felt his heart pounding in his chest. Cierra wasn't like any woman he'd ever met.

"Want to see my place?" He asked eagerly, crossing his fingers on the steering wheel, praying she wouldn't say no. He stared blankly ahead wondering what was coming over him.

"Sure, I'd love to," Cierra replied.

***

Twenty minutes later the flashy luxury car pulled into the driveway of an obvious wealthy home. The modern mansion looked peaceful nestled against the hillside.

"You live here?"

"Yes, I do," Ryder smiled.

"Wow you're in in the hills? Houses up here don't come cheap. You must be rich," Cierra breathed out.

"Kind of, Ryker said. "Would you care to go inside?"

Cierra pushed her glasses back on her nose. She didn't want to let on how awestruck she was. "This is an

awfully big house. Do you live here alone? I mean..." she
hesitated. "I know I'm not awfully smart when it comes to
men. But I hope you don't mind if I ask if you are married
or something? I mean your sister Isabella never mentioned
that you had a wife."

Ryker chuckled as he punched in a series of codes
before he opened the door. He took her arm and led her
inside. The foyer flooded with soft light. He led Cierra
down the hallway into the sunken living room complete
with vaulted ceiling and a dazzling chandelier. A white
leather sectional centered the room in front of the fireplace.

"What would you like to drink?" he asked.

"A Shirley Temple please," she said. She wasn't
sure what was going to happen, but she didn't want to think
she would let herself be led to doing something under the
influence of alcohol. Not that she ever had in the past. She
squinted and pushed her glasses back on her nose. She
knew the reason why she came. She desperately wanted to
make love to Ryker Granger. She heard all about his sexual
exploits. She heard from his sister Isabella's closest friends
about the wild frantic lovemaking Ryker was known for.
With Ryker she would enjoy sex. Ryker was the person
who could save her. He could make her forget.

Cierra sipped her drink as her thoughts consumed
her. At twenty-seven-years of age, she hid a dark secret.
The only person who knew was Enzo Rawlins. Her best
friend. It was her junior year in high school. A year she'd
never forget. Enzo had stumbled upon Cierra just after her
Physics teacher, Felix Von Bran ran his sick, cold hands

between her legs as he held her pinned to the floor of his office.

The old memory always made her feel dirty and used. As easily as the memory came, she shook out her thoughts. She knew why she'd come. Ryker was the man she wanted to create some wonderful love making memories with. She'd made up her mind. Nothing was going to stop her.

She swallowed hard and put down her glass. She walked over to where Ryker stood. "Aren't you even going to try and kiss me?"

"Beg your pardon?"

Cierra moved in close and placed her hand on his neck and pulled him in close.

Ryker kissed her back as an excited urge raced through his body.

"Ryker," Cierra moaned. "Aren't you going to help me take off my clothes?"

Instantly he began unzipping her dress. He stared at her, his face filling with admiration.

Within minutes they stood before each other naked.

Cierra grabbed a chenille throw and tossed it on the leather sofa before removing her glasses and lying back against it.

"Leather can be cold sometimes," she murmured.

"Don't worry about getting cold. I'll keep you warm," Ryker said, as he maneuvered on top of her.

The moment he entered her Cierra surged up. She closed her eyes and swallowed hard determined to vanquish that time long ago. The memory tried to surface. In her thoughts she heard herself say. "Just relax. The past is over and done with." The old memory disappeared.

She took a deep breath and felt her body becoming aroused.   And then suddenly she gasped with pleasure. This was how sex was supposed to feel she thought as she clung to him and breathed in the scent of his body. He'd chased away the bad memory.

"Oh Ryker," she purred.

Desire ripped through him at the sound of her calling his name. He traced his hands over her silky body and knew Cierra was everything he had ever wanted. He knew it was much too late for him to turn back as his body shuddered reaching its climax.

"Oh God that was so wonderful!" Cierra said.

Ryker leaned up on his elbow. "It seems you may have left out an item or two about yourself Cierra."

"I suppose you had expected me to bring up the subject of our having sex without a condom," she replied, staring back at him with her soft big brown eyes.

"Yes, we did sort of neglect that part," Ryker said, captivated by the woman in front of him He almost lost his train of thought. "But no, that wasn't what I was concerned about. I was referring to the part where you sort of missed out on telling me that you were a virgin?"

Feeling totally confused Cierra mustered up the energy to push from underneath Ryker and got out of bed. "Look, I didn't recall you're asking?"

Afraid that she would lose her courage, she started grabbing up her clothes.

He gave her a charming boyish grin. "Yeah, well that's not something a man has to ask a woman as old as you."

Cierra sighed angrily. "What a bastard," she thought reaching for her dress and pulling it back over her head. She checked the clock. It was just ten thirty. They could be back at the party within twenty minutes.

She gave Ryker a stern look. "You need to get me back to that party, like right now!"

He studied her face to see how serious she was.

As if on cue her cell phone rang loudly.

"Don't answer..."

Before Ryker could finish his sentence, Cierra checked her caller ID. She answered it. "Hi Isabella."

"Cierra, where are you? I've been looking all over the place for you."

Cierra grumbled under her breath and retained her cool head. "I just stepped outside for some fresh air," she lied. "And I got side tracked, but I'm on my way back inside."

Isabella hollered in an anxious voice. "Don't you ever do that again you hear me? Here I am listening to all these geniuses and their gibberish while they are waiting to meet you," she yelled and didn't wait for her to answer. "Well Miss Cierra, you better get your ass back inside here pronto."

"Yes of course I will Isabella. I'm on my way right now, goodbye Isabella," Cierra replied, as her head jerked up and looked straight into Ryker's eyes.

She hung up the phone. "Ryker get dressed. You're taking me back now!"

With a hint of amusement tugging at his lips. "You can be a bossy thing can't you Miss Cierra?"

Chapter 3

Ryker and Isabella had bene raised in their family home in the hills of North San Jose California. Their father, Colbert Granger had been an officer in the Army, stationed at Moffett Field back in the 1970's, when he'd bought their family home that was perched high up Sunset Mountain Road. Their mother, Lana Granger and their father Colbert had been married for thirty-five years.

Ryker pulled his car into the long driveway and realized it was loaded with cars. He glanced to the back of the house and noticed a noble, high tent had been erected. He had forgotten what day it was.

It was the last Saturday in April, the day was an annual event in his family. The day his sister Isabella Duvall hosted her annual appreciation afternoon tea. His sister was a believer in volunteering and getting others to agree with her vision. Serving afternoon tea Southern style complete with a Honey ham and roast beef were Isabella's way of gaining volunteers to work her fund-raising events throughout the year.

Well at least he knew the food would be good, Ryker thought getting out of his car and heading for the door.

Striding forth like he lived there Ryker opened the front door and immediately collided with someone.

"Oh, I'm terribly sorry," a woman yelled, in desperation.

Ryker scooped her into his arms. It was his lucky day. His heart began to thunder in his chest. "Cierra, Cierra Cantrell?"

Cierra looked up surprised into the same mesmerizing deep green eyes she had seen a few weeks before. They were unforgettable just like the man they belonged too. "Hi Ryker, I haven't seen you since..."

He finished her sentence. "Isabella's dinner party. In fact, I left you a message."

"Yes, you did," she said giving him a big smile. "But I didn't want you to feel obligated."

Ryker gave her a big smile as his eyes captured hers. She thought like he did, and she felt good in his arms. He gave her a gentle squeeze. "You're okay? I didn't hurt you or anything?"

"No, I'm fine," she nodded.

After a moment of awkward silence, she said. "Ryker, you can let me go now."

A woman's voice gave a tender giggle. "I think my son likes holding you and I must say it makes me happy to see something flash in his eyes for a young woman, besides lust."

Ryker looked up. "Hi Mom!"

Cierra's eyes widened in surprise and pushed out of Ryker's embrace. "Oh goodness, Mrs. Granger! I'm so embarrassed."

Mrs. Granger giggled. "Sugar don't be. This is like that thing they talk about in the movies, the meet cute."

"Excuse my mother Cierra, she is a romantic at heart. She sees romance everywhere," Ryker said, still standing close to Cierra. He didn't want to let her out of his sight.

"Be careful with my son Cierra, he's a big wolf. I'm sure you've heard about his reputation?" she asked but didn't wait for a response. "Anyway, just so you know Cierra, my son Ryker is screwed up when it comes to matters of the heart. But still a mother can always hope her only son will marry and settle down."

Cierra laughed at the playful bantering. She had met Ryker and Isabella's mom, Lana Granger earlier. She remembered her well because of the five-carat, diamond ring encircled in the most exquisite setting she'd ever seen on her left hand. One thing Cierra was sure of was that the Granger's had money. Their elegant lofty home perched on the highest hill in the Berryessa Hills and was an indicator of that not to mention their influential social status known throughout the Silicon Valley.

"Well Ryker," Lana Granger said in a voice with a hint of Cajun drawl. "Are you going to give your mother a hug?"

Out the corner of her eye she caught the young woman trying to sneak off. "Miss Cierra my dear," she called in a lilting, slightly commanding voice. "Don't rush off. My son Ryker needs an escort to the buffet table. You know males do like to be needed."

"Yes…Yes Mrs. Granger."

Mrs. Granger patted her son's hand. "Oh, and Ryker make sure you grab…."

"Two slices of Red Velvet Cake, one for you and one for dad and bring them to Dad's office," Ryker interrupted, finishing her sentence.

"Don't be such a smart-ass Ryker," his mother chuckled, with a wave of her hand. "And be nice to Miss Cierra. I like her," she said as she walked down the hallway.

Minutes later, Ryker and Cierra meandered down the buffet table.

"Your mother told me her maiden name is Lana Marie Toussaint and that she was born in New Orleans. She said she had you there too," Cierra said, trying to make small talk.

Ryker nodded trying to stay focus. Heat had been rising in his body from the moment he arrived, and she tumbled into his arms. It wasn't easy standing so close to her. He focused and said. "Yes, I was. But Isabella wasn't. She is a California native, born and raised."

Ryker stopped abruptly and captured her gaze with his. "Now enough about my family. I know all about them. What I don't know is why you and I haven't gotten together since that night? Did you dislike being with me so much?"

Cierra noticed the strong lines of his face were suddenly sharper. She swallowed hard and decided to be blunt. She leaned over and whispered "I just thought you were into the one-night stand thing. I didn't know you expected me to have sex with you all the time."

Her sudden revelation caught him completely off guard. "I think you are the first woman that ever said that to me," he said, putting a plate of Red Velvet cake into her hands. "Here hold this."

"You want me to take the cake to your mother?"

"No, I want to make sure you can't run off and slip away. Come on, I know a spot where we can talk," he said, slipping his arm around her and leading her a short distance away.

They stood closely together in a far shaded corner, off the patio.

"Okay, I want to know everything about you, Cierra. How many brothers and sisters do you have? What are your hobbies?" he asked without giving her a chance to answer. "So where do you work?"

Cierra smiled. "Well, I'm an only child. And since my father passed away it's just me and my mom. I work at Net-Micro Technologies, at their office over off First Street and Highway 237. I'm in Systems Administration. And I won't work there always. I have dreams for my future."

She looked up at Ryker and searched his face for derision and found none. She was taken by surprise at the sincerity she found in his gaze. It showed he was genuinely interested.

Cierra felt a warm flush creep up from her neck. Rarely did she blush, but Ryker's physical presence standing so close to her warmed her inside. She felt like she could tell him anything. She knew she could get to like this man easily. He oozed with charm, money and sex appeal. "My father and mother owned a successful real estate office," she said in a low voice. "When I was in my teens I worked there during the summer. I guess you can say real estate is in my blood. Anyway, my father was quite a bit older than my mother and the two of them didn't meet and marry until she was in her early thirties." For some reason she felt at ease being honest about herself. "She had me exactly nine months after they were married," her voice was sad. "My father died the first year I was at college and well, my mother sold the business to make sure my college was taken care of, and that she was provided for."

All of a sudden, she abruptly stopped talking, and wondered why she had told him so much. It was like she was under hypnosis standing there next to him pouring out all the details of her life.

"Forgive me for talking so much. I hope I wasn't boring you?" She asked standing there quietly.

"No, of course not. Remember, I asked you to tell me about yourself."

Ryker had always preferred sleek women but this lush abundant voluptuous woman with an overabundance of dark-hair and big brown eyes was taking his breath away.

When he finally slipped out of his musing. His eyes peered over Cierra's shoulder and caught sight of a figure coming their way.

"Ryker darling, I thought that was you. Isabella told me she thought you were here," A beautiful tall slender Brazilian woman with a heavy accent came and stood rudely in front of Cierra.

"Damn!" He muttered under his breath. It was Kalita Lopez. She was the last person he'd expected to see, he thought. She never could understand the word no.

"Give me a kiss Ryker my love, and show Kalita Lopez how much you've missed me," she said in a deep accent, that was tinged with an over indulgence of sexiness.

Cierra watched the woman named Kalita Lopez's lovey-dovey display of affection for Ryker and took it as her cue to leave.

"It looks like you're real busy right now Ryker," Cierra smiled politely. "I'll just go and take your mother that cake she asked for earlier," she said abruptly walking off.

Cierra didn't see the furious look Ryker gave Kalita Lopez.

"Damn Kalita, why is it that you don't respect boundaries?"

Kalita crafted a smile that was intended to make her look remorseful. "I'm sorry Ryker I just thought that maybe we could talk about business."

Ryker's mouth set into a frown. "I see, I'm guessing that business of yours is getting to be a little slow?"

"Yes, it has," she muttered.

Ryker glanced back at Kalita. "And why are you telling me?"

Kalita leaned in. "In the past your business dealings helped my business. One hand washed the other so to speak. I was hoping we could still help each other out. Maybe you could throw me a few odd jobs, so to speak?"

"What's in it for me?"

Kalita smiled slightly. "I saw the way you looked at your sister Isabella's mentee, Cierra. She looks radiant, fresh."

The smile on her face disappeared. She thought to herself. *"I hate that kind. You know the ones that are so unused."*

Ryker silently watched Cierra as she went into the house.

"You like her, I can tell," Kalita breathed out.

Ryker didn't say a word. As usual Kalita was her old observant self. He stared back at her with a quiet gaze.

She let a moment of silence go by. "What would a man like you want with her?"

Ryker's face went cold.

"Hold on now Ryker, I'm just repeating what I heard your sister Isabella say," she hesitated for a moment. "And do you want to know what else Isabella said?"

Ryker's mouth dropped open and then he closed it, as he looked thoughtful for a moment. Maybe she knew something. "I can tell by that light in your eyes you're dying to tell me. So, go ahead."

"What's in it for me Ryker?"

"Oh, I guess I can see what I can do to send some business your way."

Kalita laughed maliciously. "Thanks Ryker."

"And you were saying?" he asked.

"Isabella said she is trying to make Cierra into a mini me. Not to mention she is planning to do whatever it takes to keep you from ruining Cierra, the way you've ruined other ladies in the past. In fact, Isabella has commitments from a bonafide possible fiancée for Cierra and she's pretty sure she could have the two of them married within the next sixty days."

"Oh yeah, who's the guy?"

"Actually, Isabella's got two guys lined up. Collin St. Martin and Henri Allard. My bet's on Collin. You know he's that doctor's son." she hesitated. "Don't tell me you haven't noticed how much Dr. St Martin and Isabella are always talking privately together."

Instantly Ryker's face froze as he wondered. The images he conjured in his mind bothered him. "What was he supposed to do about that?" The thoughts in his mind raced.

Kalita flung him a glance while he wasn't looking. "And you know I heard Isabella say Dr. Martin say himself that he would be willing to give Isabella total freedom in planning the wedding and making sure the whole thing go off without any objections. Even from the bride," she said sarcastically. "Money can buy everything you know? Even a bride."

There was a momentary silence.

Ryker was irritated imagining his sister Isabella planning a wedding for that stupefied Collin St. Martin. Who did she think she was using Cierra as some pawn in some marriage scheme of hers?

"What's the matter Ryker," Kalita smiled knowingly. Her thoughts raced but she didn't utter a word. "Did you have plans to have a taste of that new tail Cierra for a while? By the look in your eyes I think you did."

Then all at once they exchanged looks.

Kalita swore the look he gave her sent shivers down her spine.

"Look Kalita, don't tell Isabella you told me about any of this, okay?"

"Don't worry, Isabella won't hear a thing from me?"

Ryker nodded. "Good because if I find out she did. Your business dealing with me would be over forever."

"Of course, I understand what you're saying Ryker."

"Good," he replied and then reached into his pocket and handed her a card. "Here, this guy helped me out on one of my investments and he's always looking for an opportunity to cheat on his wife," he said pressing the card into her hand. "I need to take a walk. Bye Kalita," he said before she could respond.

Ryker wasted no time hurrying inside. For some reason what Kalita had told him about his sister's plans for Cierra didn't sit well with him.

Once in the house and heading for the one place he knew his mother and father were holed up hiding from the throngs of people overtaking their backyard at Isabella's annual tea.

He walked briskly into his father's study as Cierra was just leaving.

Cierra had just closed the door.

"Hold on a minute, Cierra," Ryker said, grabbing her by the arm. "Let's go somewhere where we can talk."

Cierra sighed heavily as she followed him. For once she wished she'd brought Enzo for support.

Enzo Rawlins wasn't her boyfriend or anything serious like that. They had just made a pact years ago to be available to be each other's escort if needed.   The truth be told; Enzo wasn't her most favorite person. But he was her best friend. Enzo could be a user, but she didn't care because today had been just one of those times she desperately wished she had an ally to escape to.

"Cierra! I've been looking all over for you," Isabella called. "Ryker I'm so sorry to interrupt but I need Cierra. She is my mistress of the ceremony and she must make my sponsor announcements."

Ryker watched coldly as his sister whisked Cierra out of his reach. He hadn't been expecting that. He fidgeted uncomfortably. "What the hell," he mumbled under his breath. Feeling the beginnings of an erection. "Damn," he said in his mind. For once he was all out of plans. His brain shifted into gear. He needed a plan. But first he needed to make a quick exit.

Chapter 4

Three weeks later...

Ryker Granger took the Guadalupe exit, and marveled at the tall buildings now flanking the skyline of downtown San Jose. He made his way down Market Street and parked his car at the underground garage at the Silicon Valley Hotel. He took the elevator to the main floor and headed down a long corridor. The corridor ended at the entrance of the Imperial Ballroom.

The sign out front announced The San Jose Gladiator's Foundation Annual Dinner.

Ryker shook his head. He knew it was just a superfictional excuse for a bunch of old men and the nonprofit organization they formed decades ago to feel good about the financial support they gave to their community.

His father Colbert Granger was one of the old men and every year since Isabella was old enough to become the event planner. His father had made sure she ran things, under his watchful eye of course.

Ryker let out a sigh of relief. He knew he was early. The charity event wouldn't start for five hours. But he was a man on a mission. He had to know if Cierra Cantrell would be there.

He found the person he was looking for. His sister Isabella. She was standing at the center of the ballroom with her hands on her hips directing staff on final details. She held a seat chart in her hand and a file folder and a box.

He stood there staring.

All at once the small crowd disbursed to follow Isabella's instructions. Wearily she caught her brother's attention. "Well Ryker, I thought you'd take the hint, when I ignored your telephone calls," she said tactfully.

Ryker closed the distance between them. "I thought you were ignoring my calls."

"Well, since you are here, I guess I should make use of you," she nodded. "We've got four hours to go until this event starts. Let's put you to work."

"Always the voice of reason," he teased. "Why should I help you, sister? I know you've got everything under control."

Ring! Ring!

"Aw that's my cell phone," Ryker said. "Let me take this. I've been waiting for this call," he said walking out of the nearest exit.

Isabella let out a breath as she studied her big brother leaving.

Ryker Granger was a geeky genius born with good looks. But at a very early age she learned that her brother possessed a disciplined demeanor that some folks found overpowering. Even as a man, his manners, drive and ambition were viewed by others as being cold, distant, and calculating.

A low strange sound filled the air. Isabella looked back at the DJ station, but it was empty. He had left the room.

Isabella looked around the room. It was empty as though a curtain had descended and covered, the room taking her back in time. Back...Back.

She swallowed hard as she felt the chill hit her. The girl with the striking brown eyes laid on the hospital bed in front of her. She was pregnant.

"Isabella please... Please help me! I'm afraid."

Isabella had looked on in despair. There was nothing that she could have done.

Indira Jones had been a minnow in the ocean of life known as her brother Ryker's world. Ryker had been attracted to Indira from the start. She looked like a Paris model. Beautiful face, big brown eyes and long lean legs that didn't stop.

As with all things Ryker's business was more important to him than people. It seemed to be the thing that attracted Indira more to Ryker. She craved him like an addict craving a drug of pure pleasure.

A stab of pain shot threw her as she recalled just how badly her brother had humiliated a girl she knew a long time ago. A girl with striking big brown eyes just like Cierra's.

Lost in her thoughts she heard a voice.

A man's deep hoarse voice rung out. "Hey Ms. Isabella, are you alright? Your brother is trying to get your attention," the DJ said, glaring back at her.

"Oh, I'm sorry DJ..."

The DJ looked at her puzzled as he interrupted. "You asked me to call you Ms. Isabella and I didn't mind because I know you've got that "call me Miss Diana Ross" syndrome thing going on," he smiled assuredly. "So why can't you remember I like being called the Media Manager?"

For a moment Isabella stared at him too dazed by his abruptness to respond. "Sorry, I forgot. I have so much on my mind and you know I can get caught up in my thoughts," she tried to joke it off.

He nodded and looked away.

Just at that moment. Ryker closed the distance between them. "Isabella I was wondering if I could talk to you?"

"About what?" She breathed out.

Ryker and Isabella both turned and stared. The noise was coming from the Media Manager. It was obvious he was still ticked about her calling him the DJ.

"Come on Ryker," Isabella said, hooking her arm in his. "Let's walk back out to the foyer. We can talk there in peace."

Ryker did as he was told. Once in the foyer. He anxiously let out a sigh. "Well, did you talk to Cierra? Is she coming?"

Isabella smiled softly. She didn't have an answer to give him. She was still waiting to see if Cierra would show.

She hadn't told him the truth that she really hadn't put any effort into encouraging Cierra to be there. She went to open her mouth.

A second later, a sweet soft voice carried on the air. "Hello Mrs. Duvall, I'm here."

"Cierra! My goodness. You made it. It's so good to see you. Now remember, I told you to call me Isabella."

Ryker could have sworn his skin prickled at the sound of her voice as relief flooded him. He turned and stared. It was Cierra Cantrell. She was here. Cierra was the most beautiful woman he'd ever beheld.   He gave her his most seductive smile. "Hi Cierra."

She was wearing jeans and a soft red sweater that clung to her in all the right places.

"Hi Ryker, nice seeing you again," Cierra said softly.

"I see you're not dressed for this event yet?"

"No, I came dressed to help out. But then I'll change," Cierra said.

"You don't have to explain anything to my brother," Isabella replied.

"Oh, by the way, Isabella. You said I could bring a friend. I hope you don't mind I brought my friend Enzo. He agreed to help out tonight."

"Yes, that's fine," Isabella said as her thoughts raced. Things were looking better then she could ever hope. She glanced between the young couple.

Cierra motioned for the young man to step forward. "Enzo this is my friend Isabella and her brother Ryker."

Enzo regarded Cierra's mentor. He'd heard Isabella Duvall events were legendary. The cream of Silicon Valley was always in attendance. It was finally apparent Cierra had taken his advice seriously about moving in the right social circles. "Thank you for inviting us," he finally managed to say.

"And thank you Enzo for coming and agreeing to help us out," Isabella smiled.

Enzo laughed. "No problem, besides I am getting paid to help out and I'm making out pretty good, if I do say so." He stood there in silent amusement and gave a mischievous wink, swept Cierra into his arms and tried to kiss her.

"What?" Isabella asked with a disdained expression on his face."

Ryker turned and examined Enzo, as a muscle twitched in his face.

Isabella stared between her brother and Enzo and knew the moment was tense. As if sensing the situation. Nervously Cierra laughed. "Enzo! Isabella and Ryker don't know what a joker you are," she breathed out.

Enzo was quick with his response. "And we both know how much you love this joker."

Instincts caused her to reply. "Actually, Enzo is still joking," Cierra said, feeling she had to explain. "He's talking about my promising to pay his way to the movies, as his payment. This guy loves to see the Star Wars movies in 3D. And I promised I'd sit through them with him. There's a Star Wars marathon playing at the San Jose Theater."

Isabella spoke up. "Of course, he's talking about the movies."

Cierra took a deep breath and turned. "Enzo, you nerd! Don't embarrass me in front of Isabella and her brother."

Isabella shrugged. "Oh, don't worry. My brother Ryker is crazy about Star War movies. In fact, when we were growing up my nickname for him was the Darth Granger, because he loved going to Star Wars movies so much."

Enzo stammered, and he gushed out. "Wow, I'm in the presence of the legend himself. Darth Granger. The Ryker Granger. I read an article that your nickname was Darth Granger! Man, you are my idol. From working venture capitalist to owning your own company, to having a way with the ladies," he grinned.

"I'm the one," Ryker grinned.

Isabella breathed out "Oh God a Ryker aka Darth Granger fan!"

Enzo grinned. "Man, it's so good to meet you. I'm Enzo Rawlins by the way. Maybe you and I can have a drink later at the bar and you can give me a few pointers on that style you seem to have with the ladies."

"Pleased to meet you Enzo," Ryker said. "But I wouldn't want to be rude to your date tonight."

"Oh, Cierra doesn't mind. She knows I date other people," Enzo blurted. "I mean we have an understanding."

Ryker cleared his throat. "Somehow I think my sister probably has loads for you to do."

"Naw man, I'm sure we could sneak away and grab a drink," Enzo assured him.

Ryker turned and smiled at Cierra.

Cierra ignored him and threw Enzo a look. "Enzo you know I promised Isabella you'd help us, and you promised you wouldn't run off, talking, drinking, or making new friends."

She stopped talking and glanced between Isabella and Ryker. "Enzo is a talker if you haven't guessed."

Enzo grinned. "Cierra is right. I am, but I haven't forgotten I promised her I'd make a good impression on you Madame Mentor," he laughed, adjusting the garment bags he was carrying.

Cierra took notice. "Excuse me Isabella, where can I put these garment bags?" Cierra asked. "I didn't want to wear my evening dress since I knew you wanted me to help you set up," Cierra smiled warmly. "I remembered you said we could get dressed in your suite?"

"That's right," Isabella said, forming her plan. She knew just the thing to do to keep her brother occupied and keep that talker Enzo busy. At that moment she knew exactly what to do.

She threw Enzo a glance. "Enzo are you still interested in having that drink with my brother Ryker?"

Enzo gave a fantastic laugh. "Sure thing!"

"What?" Ryker said, shooting his sister a look.

"Good Enzo, then I'm counting on you to do me a big favor."

"Sure," Enzo smiled.

"You and Ryker can check on the bar set up for me," Isabella said. And then she explained it more in detail.

Cierra watched Isabella take charge giving detailed instructions.

Like a drill sergeant at boot camp Isabella blurted out instructions. "First I need the two of you to stop by the concierge desk and tell the manager I need his crew to start placing the donated art pieces on their display tables. How can I have a silent auction if my merchandise isn't on display? Then I need the two of you to stop by the bar and make sure they have my champagne toast order as specified and will be passed out as I specified."

"Yes, sir sergeant major," Ryker teased.

She turned her attention. "Don't worry Enzo," she commandingly said. "Ryker knows the details of my liquor order, we get the same one with this hotel every time? Oh, and I don't mind if the two of you sample a bottle of the champagne or the wine. Then Ryker can show you to my suite Enzo, and you can put the garment bags there," Isabella said, issuing out her commands, as she pushed her brother toward the exit.

Ryker knew his sister was a bossy woman. He started to protest but saw Cierra strolling along side of him.

Her face beamed as she gazed up at him. "Ryker your sister is an amazing woman. She told me the two of you are very close and that she can always count on you for anything. I admire that in a man."

Speechless. Ryker nodded his head and continued to stare back at the lovely creature standing in front of him. He stared back at her like he'd never seen a woman before.

She made him forget what he was thinking or what he was doing. Before he knew it, his sister propelled him toward the exit.

Isabella talked non-stop. "Oh Ryker, you know how I roll out these events. You've helped me numerous times, in the past. Take charge brother. By the way, don't forget to tell Enzo about your latest business acquisition. I'm sure he'd love to hear about it."

As soon as Isabella was sure both men were out of ear shot. Isabella turned and stared Cierra down. "I thought your mother said you weren't dating anyone," she snapped. "And for Christ's sake you can do better than Enzo Rawlins."

Oddly, Cierra thought. Isabella must have come up with that simple logic, from seeing the two of them together. But she'd never thought of Enzo in that way. He might have been the boy next door, because he lived next door to her mother. But Enzo had always done his own thing.

How wrong, she was, Cierra thought. It was satisfying to know she knew completely what kind of jerk Enzo Rawlins was. His plotting and scheming were the codes he lived by. He probably had no idea that Cierra knew about his underhanded adventures. Including the last one where he netted a hefty little blackmail sum by sleeping with his bosses' wife and making her pay him not to tell.

Cierra removed her glasses and blew a speck of dust off of them before putting them back on. Her eyes traveled, fixing on Isabella. "That was very interesting Isabella, you're thinking that Enzo and I are romantic like that. But sorry we are just friends."

"Just friends huh?" Isabella asked, sarcastically raising a brow. "Sorry Cierra, but Enzo doesn't strike me as a man who just wants to be a girl's friend, yours or any woman who catches his eye. If you get my drift?"

"On that we can both agree," Cierra retorted.

The two of them stared back at each other a second or two long and then broke into laughter.

Cierra felt so at ease with her. "Isabella, let me tell you my secret about Enzo. When I was eighteen, my cousin Savannah Desmond, who's a few years older than me, came to visit for the summer and she convinced me that Enzo was in love with me and wanted to marry me," she sighed. "How foolish I was then. So foolish that I believed her. Even though Enzo had never given me any encouragement that he was interested in me. Anyway, I followed my cousin and Enzo to Los Angeles. We all went to Disneyland together. It was there that I discover it had all just been a lie. It was a cover so that the two of them could be together. I caught my cousin and Enzo in bed screwing each other. I never blamed Enzo because he'd never told me he had feelings for me. But I can't stand my cousin to this day."

"Damn, ain't that a bitch and a bastard!" Isabella raved. "If I were you I wouldn't be in the same room with the man."

Cierra paused a moment before responding. "Actually, I can forgive Enzo anything. Once upon a time he was there for me when a bad situation turned ugly."

"A bad situation…" Isabella began.

There was a moment of deadly silence as Cierra glared at her. "Because of his loyalty to me back then," she said disdainfully. "We will always be good friends. And sometimes like tonight, he's my ride home," she hesitated. "Don't you think we should get started so that we can finish up here?"

The commanding tone of Cierra's voice wasn't lost on Isabella.

"Yes, you're right," Isabella said with a toss of her hair.

Chapter 5

RYKER GRANGER was in one of his silent moods as he watched Enzo down another glass of wine it was his seventh glass of wine and Ryker had been counting. They were about to empty the second bottle of wine. Enzo hadn't even noticed that Ryker hadn't even finished his second glass of wine.

He checked his watch. In an hour the event would be starting. He needed to get Enzo back up to the room and get him dressed in the suit he'd seen him take out of the garment bag and hang up earlier.

Enzo had taken great care hanging up the suit he was going to wear tonight. But he had selfishly asked Ryker if he would do him a favor and hang up Cierra's garment bag. Ryker dutifully did as he asked, especially since it gave him the chance to see what Cierra would be wearing.

The purple lace gown he'd hung up looked regal and elegant. Ryker could just imagine how striking she'd look in the dress.

One thing Ryker had figured out after talking with Enzo Rawlins for well over an hour was that he was a fool. A selfish, foolish game runner, who drank too much on an empty stomach.

"So, do you think you can help me get as lucky as you are with the ladies Ryker? Maybe even hook me up with a couple of your old throw away?" Enzo asked, his speech slightly slurred.

Ryker studied his drink. "What about your girlfriend Cierra. Won't she be jealous if she finds out you're tipping around on her?"

Enzo blurted out laughing. "Cierra…My girlfriend? Yeah, right!"

Ryker stared back and him. He needed to find out if Enzo and Cierra were an item. "So, what you're telling me is that you and Cierra are not a couple?"

"No!" Enzo laughed out hard. It was a combination of two much wine and too much ego. "Man, I want to be like you. A taker, a man who sees what he wants and takes it. I want to be addicted to women. Like, you know have a different woman whenever I feel like it."

"You are such a fool," Ryker thought. He nodded and said. "Hmmm, you do know that sort of life doesn't come with a sense of fulfillment?"

"As long as I'm pumping some woman's vagina with my third leg, then hey, I'm fulfilled," Enzo chuckled, his voice slurred.

Ryker's instinct told him Enzo and Cierra had some kind of history together. He contemplated the scenario he had in his mind. They acted more like brother and sister than lovers. But he had to be sure. "So, let me get this straight Enzo. You and Cierra are not dating. I mean she is a good-looking woman."

"Of course, she is," Enzo replied. "The thing is Ryker... Don't get me wrong. Cierra is a good-looking woman but were not like dating. Never have. We've got a protector relationship thing happening between us. Once upon a time a long time ago I helped her out when a guy got to touchy feely with her. You know what I mean?"

Enzo paused for a moment and shuddered at the memory and rubbed his brow as he shook his head to clear his thoughts. "Anyway, to make a long story short. Cierra and I kind of agreed that whoever gets married first must always invite the other one over for Thanksgiving Dinner. It is called plan A. But if neither one of us gets married and she hits forty. Then we put plan B into operation. You know marry the girl next door. And since Cierra lives next door and we grew up together."

"Okay, I get it," Ryker stated crisply.

In his alcohol-fueled high Enzo laughed and rambled. "Yeah, but Cierra doesn't know I got a backup plan. Plan C."

Ryker tempered his blunt curiosity and tried to sound disinterested. "So, what is plan C?"

"For starters, you know I love a woman with a fat bank account. And I have gotten my eye on one," Enzo blurted out a drunken chuckle. "Well her bank account isn't that big and fat, not yet. But one day it will be. You see this chick has been saving money to start her own business and I'm going to make sure it happens. Then I'm going to knock her up and make sure I do the home pregnancy test myself. Then I'm going to make sure she has no choice but to marry me. That's plan C."

Ryker rubbed his jaw. "Does this woman have a name?"

"Yeah you know Miss C plan. Cierra."

Ryker almost choked on his drink with what Enzo had just told him. Now he knew for sure he didn't like Enzo. His thoughts raced as he thought of a plan of his own. He checked his watch and then he summoned the waiter.

"Bartender, two shots of tequila," he called.

Ryker poured Enzo the last of the bottle of wine. "Enzo drink up. We'll chase the wine down with a couple shots of tequila," he hesitated. "And then what say we begin our little learning session on my teaching you a thing or two about women?"

The bartender placed the shots in front of them.

"Tonight?" Enzo asked, with a grin on his face.

Ryker nodded. "Yeah tonight, unless you've got your heart set on heading upstairs to the suite and changing. The event will be starting soon."

"No, I'm cool on missing on the event. The event was Cierra's idea anyway. If you're going to hook me up with some pussy. Then I'm ready to go."

Ryker checked his watch again, and then thought of the list of women he knew. One came to mind. She knew she'd be up for any job he offered her. He knocked back the shot of tequila.

"Enzo finish up your drinks and let me place a call. I'll be right back," Ryker said, reaching for his cell phone.

Ryker walked out of ear shot and quickly dialed the number on his cell phone. The phone picked up on the first ring.

"Hello sweetness, I have a proposition for you. Do you want some fun tonight?"

Chapter 6

AFTER spending a hectic couple of hours helping at the receptionist table, Cierra Cantrell was excited, when Isabella told her the last guest had been seated and relieved her of assignment.

The next thing she knew, she'd been assigned to dancer partner duties, alternating between the young attorney named Henri Allard and Collin St. Martin, the son of Dr. St. Martin and a new guy, named Blaze Deville.

After talking with Blaze Deville while dancing, Cierra learned that Blaze was a cousin of the Granger family and he took great pride in telling her everybody in the family thought he looked like Ryker. But Cierra didn't see it. Yes, she supposed Isabella had gotten it in her head that a look-alike of Ryker would take Cierra's mind off the real thing. The only problem was Cierra could tell the difference. Blaze was a poor excuse for a Ryker substitute.

Blaze wasn't on the same level as Ryker, not just in looks, height and manners. Still she wasn't mad at Isabella for thinking that Blaze was a substitute for Ryker. At least

Blaze was a better dancer than Henri or Collin turned out to be.

"Everyone in the family considers Ryker to be an untrainable dog. When it comes to women, I'm the gentleman in the family," Blaze stated.

Once again Blaze Deville was making disparaging remarks about his cousin Ryker to make himself look good.

Cierra checked her watch as the song ended. It was shortly after midnight.

A woman named Lavinia Albright caught Cierra's attention just as she looked up and gave her a contemptuous look.

Lavinia Albright was a rail thin woman, in her early thirties. She had ruby red frosted hair and caramel- smooth skin and a sense of style that put the Paris runway to shame.

Cierra and Lavinia had worked the front receptionist desk together earlier and became quick friends. Lavinia had confided in Cierra when Blaze arrived that she's had a crush on him for over a year.

Instantly Cierra had an idea. It was a great way of getting rid of Blaze for good.

All at once Cierra reached back and touched Blaze's arm. "Blaze come on, there is someone with a lot of charm and a big crush on you that I think you should meet," she stated, as she dragged him by the arm.

She headed straight for Lavinia.

"Lavinia Albright," Cierra softly said, in a most commanding voice. "I'm officially acting as what some may call the match maker, even thou others may call a pimp, but at any rate, I'd like to introduce you to one very single, and very handsome hunk, named Blaze Deville."

Cierra grabbed Lavinia by the hand and clasped it with Blaze's.

"Mr. Blaze Deville, may I introduce to you one Lavinia Albright. A lady whose exact words about you, when you arrived tonight, were that she thought you were the most scrumptious, and delicious hunk of a man, she'd every laid eyes on."

"Really? Lavinia, you find me deliciously attractive," Blaze grinned.

Lavinia nodded. "You want to dance?"

At a loss for words and with a big grin Blaze nodded agreement.

Cierra sighed out heavily. "There you are, I am now officially the pimp mistress of tonight's event," she muttered.

Lavinia leaned over and whispered. "Thanks Cierra. Oh, and sorry for the dirty look I gave you earlier," she said, clasping Blaze's hand tighter as she led him to the dance floor.

Cierra watched the two of them dancing and checked her watch again. She was ready to go home. This was supposed to have been a perfect evening, she thought. I was supposed to be dancing with Ryker right now just like Lavinia and Blaze.

A man's voice rose out. "Blaze is a great dancer, but he is just as conceded and big headed as the rest of the Deville family and Granger family too, I have to add. It is a nasty trait that seems to run throughout our families."

"I beg your pardon!"

"You heard me plain and clear!" A man's voice bellowed.

Cierra glanced up and standing right next to her was Ryker's father, Colbert Granger.

"Mr. Granger!"

"Colbert will do just fine," he said staring back at her.

The music changed to a slow song.

Standing so close to Ryker's father Cierra could see where Ryker had inherited his beautiful deep green eyes, and the shape of his sultry defined lips. The dimmed soft lights of the ballroom gave his smooth brown and tan skin a regal quality that added to the handsomeness of the man.

"Cierra Cantrell, come and have this dance with me and let me pay back the favor you gave me by bringing me that red velvet cake."

Stunned standing so close to Ryker's father. Cierra nodded. "Sure, I can't believe you remember me?"

"I couldn't forget you," Colbert said grinning wide, moving them onto the dance floor. "You are the young woman that brought me my favorite, a slice of Red Velvet cake and I never forget a name. Nor a pretty face attached to that name. That's a real beautiful dress."

"Thank you for the compliment," she said. "I wish that..."

Colbert smiled. "So, you got all dressed up for Ryker? Oh no, don't say a word. I saw the way you looked at him when you thought no one was looking that day at my home."

Cierra eyed him thoughtfully. "I didn't notice you that day until I brought the cake to your study."

Colbert chuckled softly. "Yeah, you were busy that day. My daughter Isabella had you running around like a chicken with its head cut off," he smiled. "But when I saw you earlier that day talking with my son, he looked happy. But later, when you brought me the cake," he paused, as if choosing his words carefully. "I could tell you were angry at him."

Cierra flushed. "I just realized that day that I was so out of his league."

"Ridiculous!" Colbert smiled ruefully. "You are far more than you think you are my dear, and you are a risk taker that is more capable than you know. I've seen you stand up to my daughter, Isabella. That takes guts and gumption and you've got it."

Cierra glanced back at him. "Thank you for that."

He studied her. Look Cierra, there's something you should know. My son has some kind of issue of opening his heart to one woman. I think he's terrified that he may find the love of a woman may be enough to fill that empty soul of his."

She heard him but didn't hear him. For some reason she just couldn't seem to think clearly. She felt empty herself. "I'm just tired. It's been a long night."

Colbert studied her for a long moment. "Yes, I can see that. Thank you for the dance, I am very grateful. It gave me a chance to get to know you better."

He hesitated. "I believe the young man you came with earlier named Enzo Rawlins, left and my son. Ryker drove his car. But I'm sure you already knew that."

"How did you know?"

"My daughter, Isabella told me. She said you needed a ride home."

"Yes," she said.

"Don't worry I have someone to see you home, Cierra, and safely," Colbert said with a pause. "But if I do will you do me a favor?"

A flash of alarm went thought Cierra.

"No…No nothing like that. You flatter an old man. An old man with a wife that has a death grip. If you catch my meaning," he said with a friendly chuckle.

Cierra laughed. "My apologies for what I was thinking. What is the favor you were going to ask me?"

"I want you to…" He paused with his thoughts. "Oh, never mind, Cierra. I supposed as a father, I must let my son grow up, and find his own way. Forget I ever said anything. But don't worry I will get you home safely tonight."

Colbert then turned and yelled. "Steele…Steele Coltrane!"

A tall, imposing, handsome brown, over six-foot tall man with a sensual quality that was hard to miss dashed forward.

"Jesus!" Cierra mumbled under her breath. Steele Coltrane looked like a ripped wonder. He was tall dark and muscularly handsome with the most mesmerizing dark eyes she'd ever seen.

"Yes, Mr. Granger," Steele replied.

"See to it that Ms. Cantrell makes it home safely," he said patting Cierra's hand before he walked away.

"Yes, Mr. Granger."

***

Ryker thought it had to be the longest corridor in the hotel as he walked down the carpeted hall leading to the ballroom. It was almost one o'clock. The event would be over in an hour. The double doors stood before him and then he opened one and stared back into the loveliest brown eyes he'd ever seen.

"Cierra, you haven't left yet?"

"No," she said her eyes holding his, as tension gripped in her stomach. "But I was just leaving."

"Alone I hope?"

"No, I'm taking her home," Steele Coltrane's deep voice replied, as he walked up and gripped her hand pushing past Ryker.

Steele Coltrane had taken Ryker completely by surprise as he stood there with wide eyes and exhausted from running almost all the way back to the ballroom. He wondered who in the hell had invited Steele Coltrane that night.

Steele Coltrane was a woman's dream and his nightmare.

All of a sudden, Isabella's voice called. "Ryker! I'm so glad you are finally here," she said grabbing his arm and leaning in close she whispered. "Come with me. Daddy is having pains in his chest. I've called the ambulance."

Chapter 7

ENZO RAWLINS hadn't a care in the world as he laid back as Kalita Lopez worked magic with her tongue.

The sun crept up against the window pane just as he screamed her name. "Kalita, baby! Kalita. Damn that was good."

Kalita Lopez was a mesmerizing beauty. The kind of woman who knew how to use her sex as a weapon, an instrument of pure pleasure, and a way to support herself.

"Enzo," she purred. "Kalita likes you. But you don't pay the rent. It's time for you to go. I have to meet a diplomat at two o'clock today. I need my rest. By the way, pick up those empty champagne bottles and put them outside in the recycle bin for me when you leave."

"What?" Enzo stared at her with hurt dark eyes and realized he hadn't seen that coming.

"Look Enzo don't be hurt. Everyone has to earn a living. You've been with me over a week now. The money Ryker gave me was good, but I've been handling you on charity for the last few days and that's because you're pretty good with that weapon you're stroking right now."

"So, you're not one of Ryker's old flames?" He asked but didn't wait for an answer. "You're a hooker."

"Hell no!" she said in perfect English.

"And you've got a phony accent too? What next?"

Kalita got up out of the bed and picked up Enzo's clothes and threw them at him. "Look Enzo, this is Silicon Valley in case you haven't noticed. Rents and mortgages aren't cheap. Now don't you have a job or something to go to?"

Enzo shook his head and then thought about it. Why not tell the truth for a change? "No, I'm sort of in between jobs," he said. "Hell, I should get paid to do what you do. I could use some fast money."

Kalita studied him slowly. His naked male form was sexy to behold. Her mind raced. Enzo was good at wielding that penis of his, like a gallant Knight on a mission. But was he sincere, she wondered.

She knew what social skills were needed to handle a job like she had. Enzo had those skills. Plus, he was good at laying down some really classy, sexy, sweet talk on a moment's notice. Not to mention that sexy thing he did with his tongue.

Kalita was good at judging people. And then she made a decision and flashed Enzo a grin. "Well…Well …Well," she said thoughtfully. "Are you just looking for a hobby to do when you get bored? Or are you serious about that making some fast money?"

"And how," Enzo said with a lascivious grin.

"You know you are a sexy stud muffin and I do know a few wealthy elderly ladies who would just get a kick out of letting you use that weapon you call a penis on them."

Enzo grew silent.

Kalita decided to sweeten the pot. "I know a company that is hiring, and all you have to do is be nice to a few women and let them see how capable you are in the bedroom," she hesitated, smiling wickedly.

She let her words sink in watching his brain digest the information.

"Are you serious Enzo? I mean about making some fast money," she finally asked.

"Hell yeah, I'm serious. Who do I have to fuck?"

Kalita spoke clearly. "Are you really serious enough that you are willing to put yourself out there, for money I mean?"

Enzo's brow shot up as the lips on his face curled up. "You are the one telling me that you know a company that is hiring. Paying steady money, and all that I have to do is, do something that I love to do, fucking?" He considered how much pleasure it would be.

"Screwing for money isn't as easy as it seems," she said. "You have to do whatever it takes. It's a business you know. You'll have overhead cost. The boss has to get paid."

He gave a smirk. "So, you're in the Ye Ode House of Prostitution business? And you'd be my pimp?"

Kalita let out a breath. "I don't like the word pimp. I wouldn't mind you calling me the Pimptress, but I prefer Madame."

"Funny, I didn't know I had agreed yet," he replied. "How much money are you talking about?"

"Lots...And I could make sure that they threw in a bottle of that Gayot Rosé Champagne you like to drink."

"Lot's ain't a number," he said lowing his brow. "You've got to interest me with actually dollars."

"Hump," she shot back. "As your Madame I would be expecting my cut, since I'm the one with the hook-up for the prominent wealthy women that are willing to pay."

"I figured as much. So, what are we talking here?"

"During the week, I'm thinking our deluxe escort services can make a few thousand dollars an evening. Who knows maybe you'd become in such demand we can have morning and evening sessions. The weekends will bring our premium prices. We can have you available for those women willing to pay extra for that much needed boyfriend experience to attend events with. You have a handsome hunky presence that I'm sure will fill out a tuxedo just right."

"Wait a minute, you're talking ten maybe twenty thousand dollars? Who's going to want to pay that?" Enzo asked.

Kalita giggled. "Women who want to be discreet," she said giving him a piercing look. "That will be minus my cut of course for hooking you up. You would be amazed at how much money woman give to charity."

Enzo thought back. He'd heard her say that word before. "Charity? What do you mean?"

Kalita only pressed her lips together and shook her head.

"I won't tell you another thing, unless you want to take this job. So, Enzo. Are you working for Kalita the Madame or do you want to go home?"

"You know I want to make some fast money," he grinned. "I'm in."

Kalita didn't believe in wasting time. "Good! I have the perfect client for your first job. She lives on Oak View in Alamden. Do you know that area?"

"Yeah that's a pretty high-end real estate area."

She giggled with her thoughts. "Good, because I don't want you to feel uncomfortable on your first assignment. Here write your cell phone number down. I'll call you once I have everything set up for tonight. Why don't you go home and take a shower and get some rest and be ready to be at your first assignment by say nine o'clock tonight. Oh, and expect to be there over-night."

Enzo licked his lips. "Sure, that sounds like a plan."

Chapter 8

"OH RYKER," Cierra moaned, floating in contentment as she felt their bodies mesh together in a spasm of passion so intense that she floated into oblivion.

The morning sun broke over the cypress trees. Her eyes flew open wide. She inhaled the fumes of freshly made waffles, fried fish, coffee, and vinegar filled the air.

"Weird dream," she muttered, sitting up in bed. She was naked.

Getting out of bed, she glanced disdainfully at her crumbled, discarded gown laying at the end of her bed. She checked the clock. It was just after nine o'clock in the morning. She staggered to the shower.

Cierra knew the fresh made coffee, homemade waffles and fried fish was surely the work of her mother, Ada Cantrell. The smell of vinegar in the air had to be because her Aunt Tilly LaSalle hated the smell of frying fish, even though she loved to eat fresh fried fish.

She blamed her exhaustion on that night, a week ago, when she was helping out at Isabella's event. Her schedule had been insane every day since.

The moment she had made it home that night. Isabella had called her and informed her she had an emergency that required her attention and that she needed Cierra to step-in and wrap-up the business affairs of the charity event.

Cierra had managed Isabella's request with ease. But hadn't had a moment to spend to herself. Or call Ryker and explain why he'd seen her leaving the charity event with Steele Coltrane. She blamed her unforgettable dream, about Ryker, on not being able to forget the look on his face when he saw her leaving with Steele.

The look he gave her had burned itself into her memory as she fell asleep. She supposed that was the reason she had dreamed about him every night for the last few days. She was sure Ryker had been jealous of her leaving with Steele Coltrane. But Steele was a perfect gentleman and had just dropped her off at home. He made sure she entered her home okay. Then she waved to him as he'd drove away.

A half hour later, Cierra was sitting at the kitchen table sipping her cup of coffee. She watched her mother and Aunt Tilly LaSalle carefully measure three round teaspoons of Earl Grey tea into a teapot and then pouring hot scalding water into the pot.

It was common knowledge that Ada and Tilly were the children of a French Creole named Sharif LaSalle. Their mother Mia had been born Mia Daisy Triplet, a beautiful maple colored African American beauty who hailed from Georgia. She made sure her two daughters attended the finest schools.

Her Aunt Tilly LaSalle hadn't been blessed with the majestic high cheekbones and sultry exotic slanted brown eyes that her sister Ada Cantrell possessed, and had passed on to her daughter Cierra.

But Aunt Tilly possessed pale skin and Titan red hair that had been their father Sharif's. Ada had the radiant golden skin she'd passed on to Cierra.

Aunt Tilly carefully carried the pot over to the kitchen table.

"So, Ada," Aunt Tilly replied. "I guess you're not going to church today?"

Ada shrugged and checked her watch. "There's still time if I change my mind. I want to see how our girl's event was that night."

Ada turned and stared back at her daughter. "Cierra, I know it's been almost a week, since that handsome young man that dropped you off at home. Who was he?"

"Ada! I missed seeing that," Tilly declared. "You told me to go to bed."

"I certainly did sister!" Ada replied, with a grin. "No need in both of us being nosy and chasing some young man away."

"Hump!" Aunt Tilly sighed, pouring herself a cup of tea.

Cierra frowned. "Okay you two, the evening was nice. I had a wonderful time. But there really is nothing to tell. The young man who brought me home that night was named Steele Coltrane. I don't know a thing about him."

Aunt Tilly turned and confronted Cierra. "Wasn't Enzo supposed to bring you home?"

"Yes," Cierra answered. "But Enzo took off with his car and I didn't have a ride home. Anyway, Mr. Colbert Granger arranged for Steele to drop me off."

Ada shrugged. "Well, from what I could see he was a real handsome man. You didn't try to get his number or give him yours?"

Aunt Tilly sighed. "Now Cierra we've been through this before. You've got to stop taking that Enzo Rawlins with you everywhere you go. I know he helped you overcome your shyness when you were growing up. But you know that Enzo ain't right in the head."

Cierra nodded and took a big swallow of coffee. Good thing it had cooled down. She remembered back to her awkward days in high school when Enzo the boy next door, had been her only friend. He had even encouraged her to try out for the cheerleading squad right up until he'd realized cheerleading wasn't her thing and that her passion was for the debate team. He was the one who took her to the debate team try-outs. She aced it on her first try.

Ada threw her sister a scornful look. "Oh, hush up Tilly, you know Enzo is Cierra's best friend. Don't say mean things about him in front of her face."

Aunt Tilly shrugged. "What! I just want to make sure my niece understands that we ain't raising no babies by that knuckle head Enzo Rawlins. Let him find somebody else's child to spread that crazy DNA he has."

Cierra rose and began picking up her plate and walked over to the sink. "I'll see you two later," she said opening the sliding glass door of the kitchen and making her exit.

Once the door closed behind Cierra, Ada turned and leveled a steady gaze on her sister. "Dammit Tilly! What a mean thing to say about Enzo. Talking about the boy having crazy DNA."

Tilly threw her sister a knowing look. "Oh bullshit! Ada, I know you were thinking the same thing."

Ada tried to look serious.

"Oh, come off it, Ada. You know that one was funny."

They both laughed out together.

Chapter 9

RYKER GRANGER sat beside his father's hospital bed and realized that his parents weren't the invincible. He also realized he envied the relationship his parents had together.

A stabbing pain shot through his father as he tried to sit up and reach out. "Ouch!"

"Dad, what are you thinking? Just lie still," Ryker said.

"I hate waking up in a hospital room," Colbert declared. "What happened to me anyway?"

"All I know is one-minute Isabella is yelling for me to come quickly because you were having chest pains and the next thing I knew you collapsed in my arms. You've been in the hospital a week now."

"Yeah, I remember that," Colbert nodded. "Did the doctors say what was wrong with me?"

"They said you were dehydrated, exhausted, and your blood pressure was running higher than normal, and they are still running tests."

Colbert reached for the blanket. "I want to pull the blanket closer," his father said and then looked around the room.

"Let me do that," Ryker said, adjusting the blanket.

His father glanced around the room. "Where's your mother?"

"Isabella took her downstairs to the cafeteria," Ryker replied.

"Hah!" His father nodded and smiled. "I seriously doubt that. The two of them probably rushed off somewhere to find the nearest Thai restaurant."

Ryker had to admit he was right. "You know it."

Colbert Granger leaned up and raised his hand. He waved Ryker closer. "Good, because there's something I wanted to talk to you about, in private, son."

"Yes, sir," Ryker replied.

"Let me cut to the chase Ryker. I'm your father and I'd like to feel that you got that Taker instinct from me. Chasing women, loving the art of doing business. You know what I mean," his father laughed out.

Ryker smiled coolly and sat in silence.

"Hell, you're a hot-blooded Granger just like me. I know you got that chasing tail gene from me, that's for sure."

Ryker read his father's eyes and a smile flitted across his face.

The two shared a laugh.

All at once Colbert inhaled a deep breath and stared back at his son. "But Ryker, by the time I was your age I was married to your mother and she was pregnant with you.

Now I know you don't want to give up your freedom. And that's why I've given this a lot of thought."

Ryker stood there staring back at his father.

"And you know what else Ryker?" He pointed to the chair. "Maybe you should sit down before I say what I'm going to say."

Ryker pulled a chair in close. "Okay, what is it Dad?"

Colbert Granger cleared his throat. "Ryker, I love you, son," he hesitated. "And I know you know all about my having your half-brother, Steele Coltrane two years before you were born."

"Dad I know all about the family history. Why are you telling me this?"

His father frowned. "I'm getting to that part Ryker, indulge your father for once and let me finish," he said with a tilt of his head. "Anyway, like I was saying that Cierra Cantrell is one really nice girl. And I want grandchildren, so does your mother and since getting married and starting a family is the farthest thing from your mind. Your mother and I discussed it and we agreed that Cierra was the perfect young woman to have our grandchildren by."

The moment was silent.

Finally, Colbert spoke. "You see Ryker, sometimes parents have to make hard choices. They have to look at their children in a way where they evaluate them to see what strengths they have and what weaknesses. Now take you for instance, you have an authoritative manner, but your disposition is like mine when I was your age. I loved to sow my wild oats too. Did you know Ryker, that in ancient times the Egyptians believed that there was danger in giving too much power to the youngest son?"

"No father, I didn't know that," Ryker replied. "What's this all about?"

"Hush and let me finish," Colbert said quickly. "You know I was thinking that your brother Steele, who's the oldest and he has a gentle disposition and he's devoted to you and me."

"He is your eldest I agree, but Steele is loyal only to you, I think, father."

"Oh, come now Ryker you know I feel you are a good son, an excellent son," Colbert said patting his hand. "It's just that I have a task that needs to be performed and I just feel Steele would be the right son for the job."

"Okay Dad, where is all of this leading?"

Colbert said slowly. "Well your mother and I had been discussing things and we want grandchildren. And so, we've asked your older brother Steele to marry Cierra and have our grandchildren and he agreed. So that's that. You won't be messing around with our future daughter in law and you need to get that through that thick skull of yours now!"

Ryker rose from his chair. "What the…"

At the precise moment his father grabbed his chest and let out a hollowing moan. "Oh! Shit, this is a big one!"

"Dad, what's the matter?"

His father screamed and doubled over.

Ryker rushed and pushed the panic button beside his father's bed.

"Nurse! Nurse!" He yelled I think my father's having a heart attack."

Between gasps for air Colbert muttered. "Ryker... My son go and find your mother!"

Chapter 10

THAT SUNDAY, after the week had passed. Cierra decided that morning to catch up on her exercise. She'd decided to just start a leisurely stroll down to the park and back. She had just walked past Enzo Rawlins driveway when she heard the noise of a car pulling alongside the curb.

"Enzo you've got some nerve ditching me that night!" she yelled before turning around. Her words died in her mouth when she saw who was sitting in the car.

"Steele Coltrane!" Cierra gasped enthusiastically, admiring the taut muscle on the arm as it rested on the side of his car door. "I thought you were my neighbor Enzo."

Steele got out of the car and walked over. A cool smile played across his lips.

The man was more breathtaking in the light of day.

"I'm sorry I just showed up out of the blue like this," Steele replied. "But I thought of nothing but you all week and I didn't get your telephone number. So, I decided to just show up and take my chances," he queried her sweetly. "You do remember I did ask you for your number and you said yes but forgot to give it to me?"

She glanced up at him as he stood there facing her. His face withheld a curious gladness among the handsome features.

Steele's features were so much like Ryker's. They could almost be twins.

Cierra felt disturbed by the expression in Steele's eyes. They were hypnotic and predatory. She knew she needed to set boundaries and let him know he was wasting his time. Her whispered voice betrayed her. "Yes…Yes! I remember saying that."

Tongue tied, Cierra felt frustrated by her own response. She decided that she needed to put some distance between them. "Look, I was just about to go for a walk. I have to go."

"Are you trying to avoid me?" Steele asked.

"I'm sorry," she muttered. "Whatever gave you that idea?"

"You are so beautiful when you lie," Steele said, smiling.

All at once Cierra felt his warm strong-arm slide around her waist. He smiled down at her. His teeth gleamed white.

"I don't suppose you'd want to go somewhere and have a bite to eat?"

Cierra stood there silently staring back up at him, conscious of the beating of her heart. From the moment he'd touched her, she felt confused. She looked away down at the jeans he was wearing. They were taut, as his thighs showed off his strong muscle tone. Bad idea, she heard her thoughts say. She looked back into his eyes. "What do you want with me Steele?"

Steele laughed. "All I want is to spend a glorious day with a beautiful woman. Have a little conversation, maybe. Tell her my dreams or get to know hers. And you're that woman, Cierra."

Cierra silently stared back at him.

"Take a chance Cierra and go out with me."

From his front window hiding behind a peek hole in the heavy curtain Enzo watched everything. He saw Cierra getting into the SUV with Steele. He was glad he'd had Kalita drop him off or else he'd never seen the two of them together.

He knew the story behind Steele Coltrane. He was Colbert Granger's other son. The son born on the wrong side of the blankets. The son that Colbert Granger didn't feel was of much importance. But his son Ryker was. He wondered if Ryker knew that his brother was visiting with Cierra.

The thought gave him ideas. Slowly Enzo closed the curtain.

***

Later that same morning, Cierra felt that Steele Coltrane hadn't been what she had been expecting. But then, finding that Steele was so easy to talk with hadn't been expected either.

From the moment they entered the cozy little restaurant Cierra couldn't stop laughing at the quirky things Steele would say.

"Damn", she thought. "The man was something special. Not just handsome he has been a great conservationist and he hadn't hit on her not one time while they were alone.

"I studied all through high school to be a magician and perfect my magic tricks. And when I went off to college in LA it's how I supported myself earning extra money.

Cierra gave Steele a measuring look. "You mean to tell me you worked your way through college?"

She had to wait for his answer as their waiter came over and poured more coffee.

The distinguished rich aroma of the Hawaiian coffee filled the air.

Steele took a sip. "Hmmmm I love the taste of this coffee. And the answer to your question is yes, I did work my way through college being a magician.

He checked his watch.

"And if you want to see if I'm any good at doing magic tricks, come with me. You are invited, and I promise I'll show you some of the best magic tricks you've ever seen," the muscles in his face relaxed. "I'm due to put on a performance in about an hour and a half."

"A magic show? With you? Today? Cierra stammered out. "I'm not dressed."

Steele gave her a cool enigmatic smile. "You're dressed perfectly. Finish your coffee and let's go."

***

From the moment they'd arrived at the *Mouse King House of Fun pizzeria* Cierra knew spending the day with Steele wasn't ordinary and she would never forget watching his fascinating performance.

Steele's magic show left a lot of big smiles on the crowded room full of children at the private birthday party.

"This day was perfect. And I can't believe how great you are with kids," she smiled while helping him carry his equipment back to his SUV.

"You had fun," Steele smiled.

She smiled. "Yes, I had so much fun. It was like being a kid again."

"I can tell," he replied, helping her get into the passenger side of his SUV.

Steele got into the driver's side

Then all at once he reached out and handed her something. "Here, I got this for you."

"Pink popcorn my favorite. How did you know?"

Still smiling Steele said. "I saw how you kept eyeing that little girl Nina's pink popcorn. That kid seemed to eat it slow just to watch the agony on your face because you didn't have any."

Cierra smiled adoringly at Steele. "You're right, I thought she was doing that on purpose too."

"Well, Miss Cierra let me take you home. I've got to head down to Los Angeles tonight. I've got to film my Magic act for a studio in Los Angeles tomorrow afternoon and I need to get me and my equipment down there tonight. If I leave now, I'll be there in time to have a good night's rest."

"You're doing a real TV show? In Los Angeles," she said but didn't wait for a response. "I love Los Angeles. It's a great town. I'd love to see it again. And I'd love to see you tape a show."

"Really you would?" he blurted. "I didn't ask you because I didn't think you knew me long enough to want to go out of town with me. But I'd love it if you went. It's a business trip of course."

"Of course," she replied. "You wouldn't mind dropping by my home so that I could grab my overnight bag?"

Chapter 11

CIERRA WASN'T WORRIED about a thing as Steele drove her back to her home. He parked his SUV across the street and two houses down from her drive way.

"I'm sure you can park in the driveway," Cierra said.

"No, this spot is fine. It was easily for me to just pull in. I don't have to worry about some car blocking me in."

"Suit yourself. Anyway, come on inside Steele it won't take but a few minutes for me to grab my things," Cierra said. "I usually enter through the kitchen door."

"No problem," Steele said following her. "Hmmm I smell an infusing aroma of a fragrant rich bodied blend of coffee. I bet you guys have an electric coffee percolator?"

"You have an excellent nose. My mother or my aunt must have left it on. Anyway, it has an automatic turn off. So, I'm guessing the coffee was recently made. Would you like a cup?"

"I was hoping you would ask."

"Help yourself, the cups and saucers are in the cabinet above the counter. Oh, and if you don't like dainty cups and saucers the man size mugs are in the cabinet next to them."

"Sounds good. I'll grab a cup while I wait for you," Steele said.

***

"What a wonderful day it turned out to be!" Cierra thoughts as she closed her overnight bag and hurried back down stairs.

"I'm all packed and ready to go," her words died on her lips.

"Hello Cierra."

"Aunt Tilly what are you? I meant it…I thought I heard someone else talking."

"Oh, I didn't hear anything. Are you sure?" Aunt Tilly asked, with a perplexed expression.

Cierra felt a pang run through her feeling something was wrong. "Was there anyone outside when you came up?" She asked, walking to the front window.

Aunt Tilly shook her head. "No, I don't think there was," she paused. "Why do you ask?"

Cierra walked out of the front door and looked across the street the place where Steele's SUV has been parked was empty. "I thought I was going to LA with a friend tonight, that's all."

"A friend? What friend?" Aunt Tilly hesitated. "You know when I came home, I had a funny feeling like someone was watching me.'

She turned and stared back at Cierra before closing the distance between them.

They stood in silence and stared at each other.

Aunt Tilly noticed the bag Cierra was carrying. "Look Cierra, baby. Don't tell me you were going to run off with some guy you just met. Especially some guy who didn't have the guts to hang around and meet your family."

"What?"

"Cierra did you hook up with some guy you just met in a bar?" Aunt Tilly asked but didn't wait for a response. "No wonder you are acting so strange," she said touching her shoulder.

"No, of course not. He was a friend," she whispered.

Aunt Tilly gave Cierra a hug. "Come on let's go back inside. How many times do I have to tell you to learn from my mistakes? Don't go picking some worthless do-nothing married guys who promise you they will run off with you. That's the key to messing up your life like I did with Reed."

Though her Aunt Tilly had never had a problem getting and attracting men, Reed Jefferson had been the one that gotten under her skin. And it hadn't helped that when they both were younger Reed had married someone else. But so had her Aunt Tilly.

Aunt Tilly paused and glanced out as if staring back into the past, watching her life passing like a movie screen before her.

Cierra hated it when her eyes held that expression. At that moment she forgot about her ruining her plans with Steele. "So, you and Reed are an item again?"

Aunt Tilly softly smiled. "Yeah, only this time I looked that man straight in the eye and I made eye contact that said, I must be the only woman in your life this time Reed Jefferson or else."

"Or else what?" Cierra teasingly asked.

Aunt Tilly laughed. "Or else you won't be putting your dip stick in my honey pot!"

The two of them laughed.

"Come on Cierra, I'll help you unpack and then I'll tell you all about the rest of my latest adventure with Reed Jefferson."

Chapter 12

THAT MONDAY EVENING CIERRA ARRIVED home at just after seven thirty and pulled into the driveway.

Enzo Rawlins was rolling his garbage can to the curb.

Cierra got out of her car and walked up to him. "Hey Enzo, thanks for leaving me stranded that night at The San Jose Gladiator's Foundation Annual Dinner. I always knew you weren't a gentleman, you jerk," she yelled.

Enzo gazed up and gave her a weak smile. "Didn't you get my messages?" he asked but didn't wait for a response. "Anyway, I felt pretty bad about leaving you like that. Look, I'm sorry. And I wanted to make it up to you. That is why I rolled your garbage can to the curb, so you didn't have to."

"Wow, thanks. I guess I can't stay mad at you for doing me that favor."

"You know I would only abandon you Cierra if I got really distracted. You know me…"

"Whatever," Cierra demurred. "By the way I don't know if you saw her note, but your mother said to tell you if I saw you that she's been spending time over at Maxwell Collins."

Enzo clapped his hands together. Things were looking better. His mother had found herself a new man-toy to keep her busy. "Abbey got a date with the Dashing Deacon Collins from the church," he said, walking up on the front porch.

Cierra followed behind him. "Enzo," Cierra said. "Why do you always call your mother Abbey? Why don't you call her mother or mommy like other people?"

He shook his head. "Because that's what Abbey likes for me to call her. As old as I am she doesn't want me running up on her with one of her boyfriend's yelling mommy…Mommy!"

As soon as he realized Cierra was following behind him like a stray puppy he announced. "Hold it right there Cierra. Where do you think you're going?"

"Ah…You know I was thinking they are still playing Stars Wars in 3D at the Jose Theater. I haven't paid you back, remember, you made me promise I would go with you."

Enzo grinned real wide, ushering her back down the porch. "Yeah, well Miss Cierra you're off the hook for owing me that favor. In fact, I ain't broke or bored any longer. So, you're going to have to find yourself another movie partner for a while. So, run on home before that

crazy Aunt Tilly of yours throws some dead chicken or
something in front of my path, and tells me she's putting a
curse on me again."

Cierra laughed. "Stop exaggerating Enzo. You
know Aunt Tilly really likes you."

Enzo glanced back at Cierra's house as if willed to
do so. His eyes went straight to the upstairs bedroom. He
saw Aunt Tilly staring out of her bedroom window in his
direction. The thoughts in his head rumbled unbearably as
Aunt Tilly watched him.

He rubbed his face. "Yeah Cierra you know me, and
your Aunt Tilly will never be friends, but I want you to
know she did ask me who was the guy that came by the
other day and left abruptly."

"You saw him?"

"Yeah, you've got that right. I saw Steele Coltrane,"
he said with a nod toward the second-floor bedroom
window. "And prying eyes are watching us."

Out of the corner of her eye, Cierra noticed the
second-floor bedroom window just as the curtain closed.
Her Aunt Tilly's room. She followed Enzo's lead and
turned her back.

"She's not standing there any longer. And it is lucky
for us Aunt Tilly can't read lips," she shrugged. "Did you
tell her his name?"

"No, it never slipped out. And I don't think she
really got a good look at him."

"How do you know that for sure Enzo?"

"Because I was watching the whole thing from my
bedroom window. I watched Steele slip out of the back

door when he heard Aunt Tilly's car park in the driveway. He hid behind that big old oak tree out back and waited until she went inside. And then he was going to head around the front of the house but a car coming down the street gave him pause. Steele then ducked back into the dark shadows and made his way back to the back yard. The next thing I knew he jumped over the neighbor's fence behind your house and that was the last I saw of him."

"Really Enzo are you serious," Cierra breathed out. "That sounds so crazy."

Enzo nodded. "Yes, it sounds crazy. But it was real. It happened right in front of my eyes."

Cierra couldn't believe what she was hearing. "Thanks for the heads-up Enzo. I think I should go inside."

"Sure Cierra," Enzo said placing a hand on her shoulder. "But can I ask you something first?" He asked but didn't wait for a response. "What kind of car does Ryker drive?"

"A Porsche Panamera. Why do you ask?"

"Oh no reason. Just being nosey," he smiled and let out a low whistle. "Now that's one flashy car."

His thoughts raced. "You know Cierra, we've been friends for years. I've always looked out for you. And all I have to say is, don't go messing around with two men at one time. Especially two brothers. He thought and said slowly. "It's not right with nature, you know that, right?"

"Of course, I know that. And I wouldn't do something like that Enzo."

His thoughts raced. "Good, because I can't watch over you all the time, especially not now. He shook his head. "Looks like your Aunt Tilly has been waiting long enough for our conversation to end."

Cierra glanced in the direction of his gaze and wondered how long her Aunt Tilly had been standing there in the open watching them.

Enzo nodded. "Don't worry Cierra, Aunt Tilly doesn't have a clue about Steele Coltrane. So, don't let her force it out of you. Keep your big mouth shut," he said teasingly.

"Thanks Enzo. I will."

Enzo turned to walk away and then paused. "Oh, and you got my cell phone number. Use it and keep in touch," he whistled low. "A Porsche Panamera. Wow Ryker sure has a really nice car."

Chapter 13

AT JUST PAST TEN O'clock that night Kalita Lopez called Enzo Rawlins' cell phone and gave him the information.

After taking a shower and changing he packed a small overnight bag and walked out of his home and loaded his car.

Growing up in the upscale Berryessa Area of San Jose, he had been like all the other kids who had graduated from Piedmont High School, with big dreams of one day starting the next big dot.com business. But part of being Enzo Rawlins was always having a back-up plan.

Enzo's back up plan always seemed to involve controlling others. Especially horny women with big bank accounts, he thought as he drove down the street.

***

An hour later, he pulled his car into the driveway of the affluent home in Oak View Estates in the rustling hills of Alamden Valley.

He thought the mansion was in typical California Spanish hacienda Style as he walked to the front door.

The front door opened promptly.

"Luanne Lanchon?" Enzo asked curiously, feeling he had to be the luckiest gigolo on the face of the planet.

"Yes, and you must be Enzo," she said. "Come on in. Oh, and I have the Gayot Rosé Champagne. Kalita said that it was your favorite," she said in her soft southern drawl.

Luanne Lanchon was a beautiful sixty-something woman with a slim build and big breasts. Her long, full black hair was laced, intermittently with silvers of gray.

"I have a fire going in my pleasure chamber," Luanne said, closing the door behind them. She walked down the dim lighted foyer like she was an imperious queen, as the tiered sheer negligée she wore flowed after her.

Enzo fell in step behind her and caught a whiff of her perfume as it hung thickly in the air around them.

Minutes later, Luanne led the way into the pleasure chamber, a luxurious bedroom suite at the far end of the mansion, complete with a full bar, a sitting area in front of a roaring fireplace, and huge sliding glass doors.

"Would you like for me to pour you a glass of your Gayot Rosé Champagne?

"Sure," Enzo replied, his eyes fascinated as they traveled beyond the sliding patio doors and saw a well-lighted crystal blue swimming pool.

She walked over carrying an empty glass and the bottle of champagne. "Here, hold your glass," she said, pouring the champagne.

Enzo watched as Luanne walked over to the bar and retrieved a bottle of Jack Daniels. She poured it into glass.

"I happen to much rather ride the Jack Daniels train, if you know what I mean Enzo. Champagne is okay, but I prefer my liquor hard, just the way I like my men," she held up her glass. "Let us toast to the pleasures of the flesh and believe me I love to get mine," she replied, downing the whiskey.

Enzo threw back the champagne and could have sworn it went straight to the head of his penis. But he didn't care, he looked back at Luanne and felt like desire was ripping through him. He looked up into her eyes and saw her staring back at him with a strange delight as she took the glass from his hand. All at once he thought he tasted a residue in his mouth.

The next thing he knew Luanne's hands were stripping away every piece of clothing he wore. They laid sprawled at his feet.

Enzo stood naked before her and knew he wasn't in charge.

Luanne leaned over and whispered in his ear. "Now that we've, shall we say broken the ice Enzo. Let me tell you what this is really about." She stuck out her tongue and deviously licked the side of his neck. "You will pleasure me, and you'd better be good. Because if you aren't, I will make you do it over and over again until you get it right? Now start licking!"

Chapter 14

THE NEXT DAY AT WORK RACED BY AS
Cierra busied herself with her lab reports.

All at once the phone on her desk buzzed loudly.
"Cierra," Kai Rivers, the administrative assistant's voice
was whispering on the line.

"Kai, what did you say? Speak louder."

"There is a very handsome man on his way back to
the labs. He wants to see you," Kai giggled. "I have seen
him before in that magazine called Silicon Valley Times.
The man is Ryker Granger. He is so handsome!"

"Oh really?" Cierra said, sitting up straight.

"Are you dating him?" Kai asked in her no-
nonsense way.

"Kai, that is none of your business."

"I'm taking that as a firm no," Kai said. "And just
so you know. When he comes back this way I'm asking
that man out on a date."

Cierra hung up the phone and sat at her desk as a
strange mixture of emotions washed over her. She thought
about that night at the charity event. When she was bold
enough to sneak away with Ryker and have sex with him.

The only reason why she'd done that was because she had thought it was the best way to get Ryker from under her skin.

The thoughts inside her head were moving full steam ahead now as she thought about why she went out with Steele Coltrane in the first place. She thought she could control her emotions about Ryker by going out with Steele. What a bad move that had been. Those same emotions that plagued her then were still real. Or were they, she thought.

She didn't have long to wonder at that moment there was a light knock on her lab door before it opened.

Her eyes widened with excitement. "Hello Ryker," she nervously said.

Ryker stepped inside the room. His gaze found hers. "Hi Cierra, I hope you don't mind my stopping by."

"No, I don't mind," she whispered, swallowing hard as she gripped the lab report tighter. There was no comparison. Ryker made her want to walk on the wild side. He was the only man who had that effect on her. She fought hard not to stare at him.

Ryker shoved his hands into his pockets. "I was hoping we could have dinner maybe a movie. I hear you are the type of girl who's willing to watch a Star Wars movie or two."

***

Hours later, after the movie had ended, Ryker and Cierra enjoyed a late dinner at Lil' Joe's, a famous Italian restaurant where they chatted and got to know each other better.

At first, Cierra tried to act like she'd had dinner at an upscale restaurant with a handsome man like Ryker a hundred times before. She sipped her wine slow and ladylike.

Then, their waiter delivered their food and she learned Ryker had ordered the lobster spaghetti.

From her first bite of lobster spaghetti Cierra thought it tasted like sex on a plate. All pretense of being a lady flew out the window as she plowed into her plate.

Ryker smiled with his thoughts, watching Cierra fork down another bite of lobster spaghetti as he sized her up. One thing was sure. The girl really loved her lobster spaghetti.

"I guess you can see I'm a pasta girl," she said wiping her mouth. "If my Aunt Tilly were here right now she'd make me put my fork down. She would tell me if I don't stop my hips are going to spread wider than they are," her voice trailed off as she looked back at him like a bewildered rabbit.

Silence.

The moment the words rolled off her tongue Cierra wanted to kick her own ass. Why did she say stuff like that sometimes and she was trying desperately to impress Ryker? Sometimes she didn't know when to shut up.

She hung her head.

It had been a long time since Ryker had to deal with a shy timid woman. He waited until she looked up and then his eyes snared her in his gaze. And then he said it without thinking. "Your hips look perfectly luscious to me. In fact, you look sexy as hell eating that spaghetti and I can't wait to..."

Cierra almost choked on her wine as a laugh escaped her. "No one has ever said it to me like that before... I mean when you look at me and say the word sexy it sounds...Good. Real good," she said, with a teasing smile.

Once Ryker had decided he wanted something there was no going back. He was willing to take things slow with Cierra. She was the kind of woman that he knew he should. He thought as he sipped his drink slowly sizing her up. "Well you do look sexy while you eat so keep eating. Besides, I heard your stomach growling earlier. I don't want anyone to think I don't feed a girl I take out on a date."

"Thank you, Ryker. By the way, I haven't had this much fun catching a movie and having dinner."

Ryker couldn't fight his natural instinct to probe. "What about you and Enzo?"

"Enzo and I never dated. Not like real dating. Of course, I go to the movies with him every now and then," she hesitated. "But well Enzo, is more like my brother."

"Oh, that's good to know," he glances at her with perception, as he poured her another glass of wine and signaled for the waiter to bring another bottle.

Ryker and Cierra continued to drink, chitchat, and enjoy each other's company.

It felt so romantic being there with Ryker. She sat there a moment her eyes locked with his. "By the way," Cierra said, taking a sip of wine before continuing. "I have condoms, in my purse. I mean just in case," she said devilishly smiling back at him.

Ryker looked back at her. "Just in case?"

The wine was going to her head. Cierra thought as she leaned in closer. "Are you going to kiss me Ryker?"

"Let's see," he said, as he covered her mouth with his.

A low whimper escaped her.

Ryker unexpectedly drew back. "I think we should leave. This is a family-oriented establishment."

Chapter 15

The next day, Enzo slept well into the evening after servicing Luanne Lanchon, the beautiful sixty-something year old with a slim build and big breasts, the night before.

He sat up in bed and stretched. He felt groggy like his mind was in a fog. Luanne had put him through a workout. He thanked God he had completed the 25-mile marathon training at his local gym, if he hadn't he wouldn't have been able to keep up with Luanne all night.

He swung his legs off the side of his bed and slipped his feet into his comfy slippers and walked into his bathroom. He headed straight to his tooth brush and quickly loaded it with toothpaste and shoved it into his mouth. After quickly brushing his teeth he turned on his shower and stripped off his pajamas and climbed into the shower. Warm water engulfed him and as he took a deep breath and ducked his head under the shower spray. He exhaled feeling his senses come back to life as he shampooed his head.

Minutes later he stepped out of the shower and ran a towel over his head then quickly dried his body. He checked the mirror his hair was a mess, but he felt like a new man. Quickly he found his slippers and headed into his closet. Finding his underwear, a shirt and some jeans he tossed them on the bed and quickly got dressed.

Just as he finished his cell phone rang and he immediately picked it up. "Hello!

"Well, Enzo it would seem you were a very good boy last night!" Kalita Lopez voice sung out into the phone.

"Oh, was I," Enzo said buttoning his shirt. "I hadn't notice."

"You know you were. You conceited bastard! But, Kalita is not complaining. Maybe a little jealous of the good time you gave Luanne. Luanne told me of your excellent performance detail by detail. You did some moves on her that I can't wait for you to use on me," she exhaled and paused. "Apparently, you were so good that Luanne gave you a little extra to show her appreciation and makes sure you return, again to see her."

Enzo chuckled. "I bet you are jealous at the sound of my getting paid extra. How much?"

"I have a feeling you already know how much Luanne gave you," Kalita replied.

"Yes, I do. But I still want to hear you say it," Enzo chuckled.

"The bitch gave you a three-thousand-dollar tip! And she had the nerve to tell me, Kalita, that I'd better give you every penny of it! The nerve of that bitch!"

Kalita started talking in rapid Spanish. It was clear to Enzo Kalita was pissed.

"Kalita! Kalita! Darling, no Spanish please! There's enough of Enzo to go around."

"Yeah, but you don't understand Enzo, that bitch wants to monopolies your time and after the blow by blow description she just gave me. I'm horny as hell," she replied, in a heavy Spanish accent tinged with an over indulgence of sexiness.

Enzo chuckled. "So, what I'm hearing you say is you need a little Enzo to make it all feel better? Right?"

'Yes, Kalita, needs her pussy licked like you licked Luanne's," she purred.

Enzo's voice softened. "You sound like you need it really bad. I mean, for me to lick your pussy."

"Oh! Yes! ... Yes! Enzo, I do. I do." Kalita moaned.

"No worries, Kalita, you've been good to Enzo, right."

"I have," Kalita replied. "I hooked you up with a job. A great paying job! A job that's paying you three thousand dollars in fucking tips for licking..."

"That's cause I'm Enzo and I'm damn good at working my tongue and stoking it where it's needed."

"Yes! ... Yes! You are!   So, Enzo's when are you going to take real good care of Kalita?"

"You've got my three-thousand-dollar tip?" Enzo seriously asked.

"Oh, yes. I got your money, Enzo. It's all right here with me!"

"Then, I'll be right over!" Enzo declared. "In fact, leave the front door unlocked, then get naked, get in bed and have your legs spread wide open when I get there! Comprender'!"

Chapter 16

    A WEEK LATER, that Monday morning Tilly LaSalle watched patiently as Enzo Rawlins pulled his car into the drive way next door. Both of their houses had been built in the 1920's California ranch style, separated by the overgrown box hedge that had been planted by Enzo's father, Carlton Rawlins, when he was alive.

    Carlton Rawlins was fond of women when he lived, and he'd planted the hedge to conceal his slipping women in and slipping women out when his wife hadn't been at home.

    Tilly LaSalle knew all about Carlton Rawlins' weaknesses because she had a few of her own and one of them was Carlton. But she gave up Carlton Rawlins cold turkey when her sister Ada Cantrell had to move in with her young niece Cierra after her sister's husband, Drayton

Cantrell, died. Aunt Tilly shook out her thoughts as she watched Enzo sitting in his car.

Enzo sat in his car a few moments and leisurely fingered an envelope that he clasped in his hand. Not bad for doing something he was good at and loved to do, he thought as he chuckled and got out of his car.

"Good morning Enzo!" Aunt Tilly called.

"Not anymore," Enzo muttered under his breath where she couldn't hear.

Aunt Tilly walked through the hedge that separated their yards. She held a black cat tucked in her arms.

"I was just letting my cat Sebastian out for the morning when I saw your car drive-up," she said. "I can see you haven't been out looking for a job."

Enzo knew better than to question her. But he suspected she had been watching and waiting for his car.

For a moment he couldn't tear his gaze away from the cat, she held in her arms. He watched her slowly stroke the cat.

"You know Enzo; Cierra has a job. She gets up and goes there Monday through Friday. You should go out looking for a job. It pays a respectable paycheck you know?"

"I wouldn't worry about Cierra, Aunt Tilly," Enzo said briskly.

Aunt Tilly gave Enzo a knowing look. "You know what I'm really interested in knowing?"

"No not really," Enzo said, shaking his head and taking satisfaction in how upset he was making her.

Instantly Sebastian, the cat purred loudly and tilted his head and stared back at Enzo.

Aunt Tilly gave a slight chuckle and gave a soft purr as she stroked the cat. "Don't toy with me Enzo. You know how upset Sebastian gets when mommy is pissed."

Enzo frowned. "Okay, fine. What is it you really want to know?"

"First of all, why is it that you reek of sex? And another thing is, did Cierra meet a young man named Steele Coltrane at The San Jose Gladiator's Foundation Dinner that the two of you went to?"

"Steele Coltrane, no that name does not ring a bell," he said.

"Are you sure? He's Colbert Granger's other son and I saw him drop Cierra off that night."

"Oh really?" He asked, studying her for a moment. "Now that I recall, I think he did give Cierra a lift home."

"I thought as much," she said, her posture changing. "You know, both of Colbert Granger's sons favor each other don't you think?"

"Huh, I ain't into men, Aunt Tilly. I hardly notice."

"Damn Enzo, I know that. I just meant that they are both tall, imposing men like their father."

All at once her eyes lit up with a revelation. "I just thought of something. Their eyes are different. Steele has dark eyes and Ryker has the deep green eyes, like his father, Colbert. Yes, now I see."

"Yeah, you're right. Steel does have dark eyes and dark coloring," Enzo shrugged. "So still when I picture them, they seem the same yet different to me."

"That's because they're sons of Colbert. They are brothers. They've got that brother look thing going on," Aunt Tilly declared.

"On that we will agree. Well, if you done with me. I'll get going," he replied.

"I haven't asked you the other thing yet," Aunt Tilly said.

"Well, what is it?"

"Why didn't you look for a nice girl to hook up with the other night? You know you should get started getting married. You won't be young forever."

Enzo was surprised by the concerned tone of her voice. "Yeah, too bad. Well, I'll tell you what. I'll keep having sex until I find the right one who's willing to give me a good time in bed and marry me."

"Just as long as it ain't screwing my niece Cierra. I truly don't give a damn. But be careful Enzo. One day your luck might run out and you might find yourself poking that penis of yours into the wrong honeypot and some nasty stuff might be stuck all over you."

Enzo snorted out a laugh. "Good one Aunt Tilly. My getting me some good and nasty stuff stuck all over my penis is usually what I'm normally trying to find when I'm out screwing in the first place."

He laughed again.

"Oh, go, and take a hot bath Enzo and wash that stench of sex off of you."

He sniffed himself. "I bet that smell makes you miss the good old days of your youth, doesn't it Aunt Tilly?

Back then you knew what it felt like to have a man on top of you."

Aunt Tilly let out a sigh of relief. And gave a knowing smile. "You're a rude and impertinent asshole Enzo," she hissed out. "Your father had manners. Too bad he didn't pass them on to you. It's about time I fed Sebastian," she replied rudely, turning and slipping back through the box hedge.

Suddenly she did miss the feel of a man inside of her. Unbeknownst to Enzo she wasn't as out of touch as he thought. And she knew where to find the perfect partner who'd like to share in a little fun.

Chapter 17

RYKER KNEW THAT CIERRA WAS in an inebriated state when they left the restaurant almost two hours ago. Now it was a half past midnight as he gunned his jet-black Jaguar up highway 80. In the distance the lights of Sacramento Valley loomed behind him as he watched her sleeping in the car seat beside him.

"This is mine," he muttered under his breath as his hand stole a feel of her soft silken thigh as she slept. He had a hard-on a mile long, but he could wait. He was patient. If all went well with his plans she would understand his plan and agree.

As Cierra slept Ryker's mind drifted back in time to another time and another woman. It had been five years ago, but it seemed like a lifetime since Indira Jones had died and taken her betrayal to her grave in her self-induced overdose.

Ryker swallowed hard surprised by how clearly the memory unfolded...

It was the day he'd discovered Indira Jones, the woman he was supposed to marry, in bed having passionate sex with a man he had never suspected.

He couldn't get the image of Indira out of his mind. Like mother like daughter, he had thought then. Watching her face contort passionately as she climaxed.

"Damn that was so good," Indira yelled, until she noticed Ryker standing there staring.

Instantly Indira grabbed the sheet and pulled it around her. "Ryker...Oh my God!"

Indira Jones was rich, beautiful, and spoiled. Her father was Thames Jones, the owner of Jones Discount Electronics, a major player in the West Coast Electronic business.

Ryker felt like a fool. Right before his eyes she had cheated on him. He heard rumors that Indira was just like her mother Goddess Jones, a nymphomaniac. For some he had always dismissed them as just the ramblings of jealous people.

Now he was faced with the scandalizing truth. Disgusted, he turned to leave the room as Indira followed quickly behind him holding a bed sheet rapped around her.

She threw her arms around him and yelled. "Ryker! Ryker I'm so sorry. I swear it was only this one time. Please don't call off our wedding. I promise I'll make sure my father gets you the contract."

The betrayal had hurt, but now knowing that she thought she could buy him and get him to marry her, hurt even more. He turned around and stared back at her.

India's big brown eyes swelled with tears. "Ryker I'm so sorry, but you're not innocent in this and you know it. I only did this because I saw you with Kalita Lopez."

"Spare me the details," he replied.

With her head held high she started to shake. "I'm pregnant and the baby is yours. You have to marry me."

"No Indira, I won't marry you. Why don't you get your friend in the bedroom to marry you? He looks like the marrying kind of guy," he paused. "But then I'm not sure his wife would give him a divorce," he said turning and walking away.

"You'll be sorry Ryker! You just wait!"

Indira kept her word. And her married lover had helped her purchase the drugs that she had overdosed with and lived to regret it.

Ryker made sure of that after hiring a private investigator to determine who had supplied Indira with the drugs she had used to overdose. The dealer who had purchased them for her married love gave up the name all too willingly for the right sum of money.

Ryker took a deep breath and brought his thoughts back to the present, in less than an hour he would be in Reno, Nevada. The best little city in the world, Ryker smiled contently. He had it all planned out as he drove down the highway. He knew what he wanted a marriage of convenience fully equipped with a prenuptial agreement.

Now all he needed was to figure out a way to get Cierra to sign it.

Chapter 18

THAT NEXT MORNING, THE SUN WAS
creeping over the sliding patio door, when Enzo's face
contorted into a rage of passion as he grunted out
satisfaction. He knew he had to be the luckiest man alive
and that Luanne Lanchon had to be the horniest woman
ever, as he grinded her woman's body on his cock.

Then they both moaned out wild groans together as
they climaxed.

"That was so incredible!" Luanne breathed out.
"Damn you have an impressive cock Enzo!"

"Thank you," he replied, in a satisfied husky voice.

Luanne leaned up on her elbow. "Just so you know,
I'm going to put you on my calendar as a regular. You
passed my test for excellent raunchy sex and I must have
you on a regular basis."

Enzo grinned wide.

"I wouldn't smile so fast if I were you lover," Luanne said shaking her head. "I'm rich and I can pay your price. But I have a sleaze factor that's a mile long and it comes with a triple X rating," she said matter-of-factly.

Luanne stared at him with a long intent smile. Then she decided to see what his reaction would be as she leaned forward and touched her index finger to his lips. "And I like a threesome every now and then. So, what do you think? Can you handle something like that Enzo?"

Enzo smiled even wider. "I'm assuming you mean another woman?"

"Of course, darling," she said.

"Then you know I'm up for the challenge. Put me on your schedule."

All at once Enzo's cell phone rang. He looked back at Luanne but didn't pick up.

Then the telephone beside Luanne's bed rang and she looked down at the caller ID.

She threw Enzo a scornful look. "Damn, looks like your Pimptress is looking for you. I'd better pick this up. I don't want to get on Kalita Lopez's bad side."

The telephone rang out again.

Enzo crawled into the middle of the King size bed and looked back at Luanne's face.

Luanne reached for the cordless phone and clicked it on.

"Hello Kalita," she replied, knowing what to expect. She then leaned back against the bed and squeezed closer to Enzo.

"Hello Darling," Kalita said in a soft accent. "Was Enzo sexy enough for you? Did he go down on you my love and give you much pleasure?"

Luanne reach over and caressed the muscles on Enzo's chest. "Yes, Enzo gave me plenty of oral sex and he is a joy to ride. In fact, I quite enjoyed our time together and I can assure you I will be using his services again real soon."

"Excellent! But you do know why I'm calling?" Kalita asked.

"Yes," Luanne assured her. "I know my time with Enzo is up. I was just going to feed him and send him home."

"Good, I know you understand I must make sure Enzo gets his rest," Kalita spoke softly into the phone. "Then I'll let you feed him. I'll talk to you soon Luanne."

Luanne clicked off the remote, laid down the phone and lowered her head between Enzo's legs and serviced him.

Enzo threw back his head and moaned loudly.

***

At four o'clock in the morning Enzo awoke. The loud snoring of the woman lying beside him had finally got to him.   The reality of his fantasy life of having women pay him for his favors was proving to become an exhausting and lonely reality.   He loved fucking women. That one thing was for sure. But at the end of a long night he didn't love listening to the loud snoring. Grabbing his pants and his cell phone, he tiptoed out of the room and made his way out to the balcony.

The early morning sky was dreary and brought out a pang of loneliness. Fumbling for his cell phone he strolled through the numbers on his contact list and quickly dialed the number.

The number rang four times and then went to voice mail.

"Hello Cierra, it's me Enzo. I know it's late. But I was thinking about you and decided I'd call and check on you. Call me back and let me know you are okay."

Enzo hung up and sat their staring out at the outline of the hillside as dawn slowly crept in view.

Chapter 19

AT ONE O'CLOCK THE NEXT AFTERNOON,
Ryker stood outside of the bathroom, trying to convince
Cierra to come out of the bathroom.

"Listen Cierra, when you went in to take a shower
didn't you notice you were fully dressed."

She took a good look at her clothes lying on the
floor of the bathroom. She had taken them off herself just
before she showered.

Ryker's voice called threw the door. "Just think, if
we'd done something they would have been off."

Cierra stood on the other side of the bathroom door
and realized his logic was right. But simple logic was just
that, simple logic. She could hear her Aunt Tilly's voice
telling her how some men could lay a mind trip on you so

fierce that he made you believe he was telling you the absolute truth. She wondered if this was one of those times.

"Look Ryker I know I had too much to drink yesterday. But how can you explain my being here in a hotel suite and where did you say we were again?"

'We are at the Hotel in Reno. But like I said earlier, I can explain everything. Just come out of the bathroom," he replied. "Aren't you hungry?"

"Yes," she answered.

"Good, because I ordered room service. We'll eat and talk."

At just that moment a knock sounded on the door.

"Room Service," a waiter called.

Instantly, Cierra came out of the bathroom and chewed her lip. "I am hungry," she said, wet from her shower. She pulled the bathrobe tighter, and pushed her gold rimmed glasses back, as she watched the waiter setting the table.

Ryker watched her with a red-hot passion. She was an incredible woman. She intrigued him. This was no woman that he played games with. He wanted like he'd never wanted any other woman before. With this woman he had to take his time.

Their waiter laid out a fine linen table cloth, linen napkins, and a crystal vase with a red rose. There was an incredible spread of food consisting of; omelets, waffles, fresh strawberries, sausages, bacon, and a salmon in a creamed dill sauce. This was served with fresh orange juice and a silver pot of coffee.

"My goodness," Cierra said. "I hope you don't expect me to eat all of this food. I'm a healthy-looking girl but I can't eat all of this," she said lifting her eyes searching his.

"No," he chuckled, as he walked over and let the waiter out.

Cierra sat down at the table and began filling her plate. She started to eat, amazed at how hungry she was. She brushed back a strand of her thick hair and poured a cup of coffee.

Out of habit she poured him a cup. "I'm sorry, I didn't even ask if you like coffee."

"Oh, honey I like whatever you're pouring," he said with his thoughts, staring back as her breasts poured out of her robe.

"I love coffee. In fact, I love everything I see," he answered.

Cierra followed his eyes to the opening in her robe and with modesty she tightened her robe around her. "I rinsed out my bra and panties in the shower with me. I squeezed them out with a towel but I'm afraid they won't be dry for a while," she said with a nervous tone in her voice.

"Let me smooth your nerves. Don't worry. You are safe with me. Besides, we haven't discussed the real reason why we're here. For now, let's finish eating and then we'll talk."

They chitchatted about nothing for a half hour. Ryker worked hard to put her at ease.

Finally, he watched Cierra put down her fork.

"It's been fun talking to you. I didn't know you had such a sense of humor," Cierra smiled.

"Thank you," he replied. He decided for the moment he'd change the subject. "Well I guess now it's time we talked about the real reason that we are here. My sister thinks she is like that famous matchmaker to the Geeks of Silicon Valley, Eris Simeon?"

They both laughed. Out.

"And how I know it," Cierra laughed, pushing back her gold rimmed glasses.

Something told her to hold back the truth from Ryker. Was it her intuition? Could she trust him? She paused for a moment and nervously laughed.

"I'm supposed to be on a date today with Collin St. Martin," she stopped laughing. "I could call him and tell him it's cancelled."

Ryker shook his head. "No…No I don't think that's a good idea, he said. "Besides, I guess by now he's probably called my sister Isabella and begged her to not to call his father. You know Collin is afraid of his father Dr. St. Martin?"

Cierra nodded knowing he spoke the truth.

"That's probably why Isabella isn't burning up your cell phone calling right now," he chuckled. "She doesn't want Dr. St. Martin to know."

Cierra grew silent and played with her glass of orange juice. "Look Ryker we have played a wonderful game of let's run away together. But life isn't a game. We all have to play the part of being serious at one time or another. And well I'm afraid. I need to get serious. I've got to choose Henri Allard or Collin St. Martin to marry."

"That sounds like something my sister Isabella put into your head," he laughed.

A frown creased her brow. "Isabella is right you know. I'm not getting any younger and Henri and Collin may not be the greatest catch to you, but they are not riff raft. Your sister Isabella has told me that more times than I want to remember. Anyway, she also told me I have to have an ambition in life and she's right."

"Yeah that's Isabella's motto, marry rich, become a prominent wife, have a beautiful home and beautiful children. But I bet she didn't tell you that you won't have a cute kid if you marry Henry or Collin."

"What are you talking about? Henry and Collin are very handsome men."

Ryker blurted out a laugh. "Everybody knows Henri Allard had a nose job and a chin implant when he was fourteen. And Collin St. Martin is had a hair transplant. He's already pre-maturely bald and he did have the beginning of his father's hanging jowls, until he had a little face lift a year and a half ago."

Cierra squirted out a laugh as she took a sip of her orange juice. "That was so cruel Ryker. True but cruel," she said composing herself. "I didn't know about them until I saw my assistant at work Kia Rivers. She showed me a before and after photo of them."

Their laughter filled the air.

All at once Cierra's laughter ceased and her face was solemn. "Ryker, sometimes we are expected to do the unexpected."

"Oh, what do you mean?"

She shrugged. "I'm only telling you this because I think I can trust you. Last night the only reason why I went out with you was because I wanted a last moment to be happy. Call it my last spontaneous moment when I did something I wanted to do rather than something that was expected of me to do. Anyway, just so you know, when I get back to San Jose I'm going to make it a point to start dating Henri or Collin seriously."

He was as placated by the evidence of her trust. He was silent for a moment. "Do you want to tell me the reason why?"

"I don't know if I should really tell you what's really happening in my world."

It was obvious that she needed to talk. He gently asked more questions. "Is it about your family? Your mother or maybe your aunt? By the way you did say your aunt's name was Tilly, right?" He asked but he already knew the answer.

"Yes, my aunt's name is Tilly. Why do you ask?"

Ryker leaned over. "I don't want you to think that I was prying but I heard your Aunt's voice call out on your cell phone earlier while you were in the bathroom, "he said. "She said Cierra this is Aunt Tilly pick up the phone. The power on your cell phone must have died because she stopped calling."

Cierra sat in silence for a few moments at the mention of her aunt's name.

Ryker studied her face. He felt the change in her immediately. It was obvious her aunt Tilly had a lot of control over her. "It looks like she likes to keep tabs on you more than your mother. Do you want to talk about it?"

Cierra felt her heart beat frantically. She took a deep breath and toyed with her glass of juice. She took a sip and took her time talking. "You might as well know I wanted to spend last night with you and feel like I had a say in my life. But in reality, I'm living on borrowed time."

"What?" He reached out and took her hand in his. She brought out the protective side of him. "Is anything wrong?"

She shook her head. "No Ryker, it's not like I'm dying. It's nothing bad like that. But it is bad."

"Where does your aunt Tilly fit in all of this?"

Fear clouded her gaze. "My aunt Tilly loves to play cards. Poker is her game of choice and she's really good at it sometimes. But other times she's not. She's the reason I have to marry soon."

Ryker watched her as she disengaged his fingers from her hand. Something was on her mind.

She took a deep breath. "You see, unbeknownst to my mother, her sister, my aunt Tilly owes a loan shark two hundred thousand dollars."

Her head jerked up and she looked back into his eyes. "I don't know why I'm telling you this. But I have to get serious about Henri or Collin and real soon."

"Why?"

Her eyes were clouded over. "Well, because you see my aunt Tilly plays cards with Collin's father Dr. St. Martin and Henri's father Judge Allard."

"And she owes them the two hundred thousand dollars?"

"Oh, I don't know. All I do know is that I've been given a choice here. Your sister Isabella doesn't know she's just a cover. A cover for two men who I suspect as scheming to marry off their sons. Anyway, she maybe just a cover for my aunt Tilly too."

"Oh, and why do you say that?"

"Because someone has agreed to pay off the loan sharks. Or they are the loan shark, if that makes any sense."

"Did your aunt tell you if she suspected that the loan shark was Henri's father or Dr. St. Marin?

Cierra shook her head. "No, she swears it isn't either of them. But I'm just guessing it has to be one of them. Because what I do know is that I received a certified letter telling me that if I did provide the bank with my marriage license in ninety days that my Aunt Tilly's debt will be erased, and my aunt would quick deed over her interest in the home to my mother Ada Cantrell if I do."

"Do you believe them?"

"Yes, I received a certified letter from First California City of Angels bank guaranteeing payment in full for the full amount of the loan by cashier's check. And I even called the bank to find out if it was a hoax. And they assure me it was legitimate. I even tried to find out who authorized the payment and was told by the bank that the payment source was The Corporation known legally as Anonymous, Inc."

Ryker nodded. "And what will happen if you don't?"

"The letter said that if I don't provide proof of my marriage certificate in ninety days the loan source known as Anonymous, Inc. had instructed them to start foreclosure. And that will mean that my mother Ada, my aunt Tilly and I will all be put out on the street."

Ryker's gut twisted. He needed to be honest with her. He knew far more about her situation than she realized. He was grateful she'd been honest with him. At that moment he wanted to give her aunt Tilly a lecture she wouldn't forget.

He had to sort things out. But first things first. Cierra would need a change of clothes while they stayed in Reno. And what woman didn't like to go to the mall. The Meadowood Mall just off of South McCarran Blvd should have everything a girl needed. Not to mention he knew a lawyer that had an office close by.

He took her hand in his and looked deep into her eyes. "Don't worry about your aunt Tilly, the money that she owes, or anything," he assured her. "Do you trust me Cierra?"

She nodded. "For some reason...Yes."

Ryker smiled and let go of her hand. "Well good then," he said nervously stalling for time. "Oh, and pour me another cup of coffee please.'

Cierra did as he asked and poured herself more coffee too.

"Thanks," he said taking a big sip, and then placed the coffee cup down.

Silence lingered between them.

All at once Ryker reached grabbing her hand. "Marry me!"

Cierra was stunned speechless. She bit her bottom lip as her thoughts raced. Ryker was everything she'd ever dreamed a man to be. He was handsome, rich, tall and strong. And he had a dangerous quality she found irresistible. Not to mention his fabulous social standing too. Guys like him could never be serious about Geeky nobodies like her. The reality of their life together could make her dream marriage with Ryker a nightmare.

"Why?"

"Because I protect those that belong to me Cierra. You and your mother deserve that. Now, your aunt Tilly needs to go to gamblers anonymous."

Before she could say another word, he reached into his pocket and pulled out a finely made gold ring with three precise cut one carat diamonds centered in it.

Her breath caught in her throat at the size of the diamond. "Whew!"

"I'm serious Cierra. I want you to marry me. Today."

"Here in Reno!" She barely recognized her own excited voice.

"Cierra, I need a wife and I want you...." He paused and reached for her hand. "No, I need you to fulfill that role. I know you are the only woman who can do it."

It took her a moment to catch her breath. "Wait a minute!"

God Ryker was moving fast. She thought she saw a glint of triumph in his eyes. Things were moving too fast. Cierra rubbed her forehead and tried to think.

In one moment, she stared again in his eyes. Ryker knew exactly what he was doing. He knew the effect all of this was having on her.

Her voice finally cracked out of her mouth. "Okay, I'll marry you on two conditions. That we have two weddings, the one here in Reno and one with our family."

"Okay agreed," he said quickly drawing her into his arms.

"No... No," she said pushing out his embrace. "Not so fast. That one stated as a two-part statement but it was only one of the conditions."

"I'm listening," he smiled hungrily.

"You must let your sister Isabella put together the wedding for our family and I want you to fly Isabella and my mother, Ada here today to witness our wedding, today."

Ryker smiled. The future Mrs. Ryker Granger was one bossy fine woman. "I've got to admit it, Mrs. Granger. You flipped the script, wanting my future mother-in-law and my sister Isabella to be here. But if it makes you happy so be it!"

He kissed her and then stopped. "But I have a couple condition also," he said with a glint of triumph in his eyes.

"What?"

"I get to tell Isabella and your mother to keep our wedding a secret until after we have the wedding for the family."

"Whew Ryker that sounds so cruel."

"I've got to get something out of this. The chance to see Isabella keep a secret of this size will make me so happy."

He walked over to her, he said. "Perhaps you should go and get dressed. We've got a lot to do today."

A thought struck her. She pressed her lips together. "What was the other condition?"

He didn't say anything.

Cierra paused waiting for a response from him.

He waited a moment before answering. "Just so you know we did make love last night. Who knows you just might be carrying my child right now. Above all, I want you to be happy and safe Cierra. And the safest and best place for my woman is married to me and right by my side."

***

After seeing Ryker take off to use the hotel business center. Cierra sat about searching the room for her cell phone. She'd forgotten where she placed it when they first arrived.

She picked up the phone in the hotel room and quickly dialed her number. Her cell phones soft hum rung out over the room. Quickly she rushed over and retrieved it. It was wedged between the pillows of a chair. She checked her messages.

"I don't believe this," she said to herself. There was a message from Enzo.

Instantly she hit redial and the phone shot to voice mail.

"Hello Enzo," she stated timidly. "You won't believe where I'm at. I'm in Reno," she took a deep breath. "Anyway, I got your message and I just wanted to call you back and let you know I am doing fine. In fact, I'm going shopping with Ryker this afternoon. Can't wait to fill you in on the details. Talk to you later, bye."

Chapter 20

THERE WERE TIMES WHEN ISABELLA DUVALL wished she'd married a man who owned his own plane and that Saturday afternoon was one of them she thought, as she retrieved her oversized luggage from baggage claims.

At least her seat had been in first class she thought as she maneuvered her way out of the Reno Airport with her overnight bag in tow. She saw the sign of limousine driver held up with her name on it and walked over.

The limo driver took her bag and then opened the rear door of the car.

Isabella smiled at him as she got in. Her smile quickly faded as she sat down.

"Mrs. Cantrell? What are you doing here?"

Ada leveled a surprised glance. "Hello Isabella, I don't have any idea why I'm here in Reno Nevada. Do you?"

Isabella studied Cierra mother's face. Ada Cantrell had blessed her daughter with the same majestic high cheekbones and sultry exotic slanted brown eyes that she possessed.

"I'm sorry, no I don't. But I have a feeling we'll both find out why very soon."

Chapter 21

AT FOUR O'CLOCK THAT AFTERNOON Enzo Rawlins felt like a kid sneaking back home, as he turned down the familiar street in the old Berryessa neighborhood he called home. He had to make a quick swerve and an abrupt stop when he notice old lady Johnson, who lived down the street from him tugging her silver utility shopping cart across the street.

"Do you need a hand, Mrs. Johnson?" Enzo called.

"I'm fine! Go on about your business, Enzo." She yelled back, as she continued pulling her cart.

He watched her pull her cart past an SUV and continued home. He pulled into his driveway and turned off his engine. The tranquil sound of his peaceful Berryessa neighborhood sooth him.

All at once the sound of his cell phone filled the air and broke his moment of silence. He checked the caller ID. It was Kalita Lopez.

"Hello Kalita."

"Hey Gigolo where you at?"

"I dropped by home for a minute. Don't worry I know my way back."

"Good then I won't keep you," Kalita said before hanging up.

Enzo checked his messages before getting out.

He'd waited long enough for Cierra to call him back again and sure enough he had missed her call. He pressed the redial.

The phone picked up.

"Cierra, baby I'm sorry I missed your call."

"Hello Enzo, old friend. Do you miss me terribly?" Cierra asked.

"Terribly my old friend," his voice shook with sincerity. "I got your message, so you went shopping. Did you buy up the mall?"

"Oh yes I did."

"They've really got a mall in Reno?"

"Very funny Enzo, you know they do," she laughed.

"I hope their prices are cheaper than New York or Paris."

Cierra breathed out anxiously. "Oh Enzo, gosh there is so much to tell. I'm about to burst trying to keep my mouth closed."

He laughed. "I figured as much. You know your secret is safe with me. Now tell me what it is."

"Enzo, all I'm going to say is that I bought a wedding dress today."

"Ryker?"

"Yes, how did you know?"

He chuckled softly leaning against his car. "Ryker is the kind of man who knows what he wants and goes after it," he said speaking as if he knew the man thoroughly.

Cierra breathed out. "You know about my life Enzo. You and I have always been so close. So, do you think I'm doing the right thing Enzo?"

"I have total faith in you Cierra," he said.

"Thanks Enzo, I needed to hear that. So, what's up with you?"

"Oh, I'm just keeping busy," he lied, and changed the subject. "So, the next time I see you, you will be Mrs. Ryker Granger?"

"Yes, I hope so."

"Good, then I know you need to get some rest for your big day. So, I'll see you Mrs. Granger when you get back."

 He looked up in surprise and spotted Steele Coltrane. He was holding an envelope.

"Hi, you're Cierra's neighbor, right?"

"Yes, I am," Enzo mumbled."

"Hi, my name is Steele Coltrane. Could you give Cierra this card for me when you see her," he said handing him the envelope. "I seem to keep missing her."

Enzo looked at the card. The envelope wasn't sealed.

Steele followed his gaze. "It's nothing urgent. It's just a card saying I apologize. There's nothing else in it."

"Sure, I can give her the card."

"Thanks, I didn't catch your name?"

"Enzo. Enzo Rawlins."

"Thanks again, Mr. Rawlins," Steele said turning and walking away.

Out of the corner of his eye Enzo watched Steele walk over to his SUV, at that moment he realized the vehicle had been sitting there for a while, he had seen it earlier.

Chapter 22

STEELE COLTRANE GOT INTO HIS SUV and stared out of the tinted windows. He glanced back at Cierra's friend Enzo Rawlins.

What kind of man was Enzo to only be friends with a woman as beautiful as Cierra Cantrell? It was obvious Enzo Rawlins had long resolved himself to only be friends with her.

At that moment he hated Enzo Rawlins for being as stupid as his baby brother Ryker Granger.

He opened his glove compartment and noticed the gun he kept there. His thoughts cleared instantly. The look of the cold back gun always brought his focus back to reality. There was only one person in the world he really hated. His baby brother Ryker.

He closed his glove compartment. He needed a plan. He checked the clock on his dashboard. Reno Nevada was a four-hour drive away. There wasn't enough time to make it there that night. His thoughts raced as he drove off from the curb.

Chapter 23

THAT EVENING CIERRA SAT STARING AT the reflection in the mirror and wondered how fast life could change.

Suddenly, her eyes caught the sight of the pile of designer dresses she had thrown across the bed and the vast array of shopping bags filled with designer shoes and accessories she'd allowed Ryker to help her shop for. She knew without a doubt her life would never be the same again. She thought back to the moment he had kissed her, and she knew she'd agree to anything he asked.

A knock sounded on the door.

"Cierra have you finished dressing yet?" Ryker's voice asked calling from beyond the door before he opened it.

"I'm almost finished," she replied, remembering her promise to him to be ready within the hour.

"No problem," he said. "I thought perhaps you wouldn't mind meeting me downstairs in the White Orchid Restaurant?"

"Oh, you made reservations?" she asked.

"Yes, I did, and I don't want to lose the reservations," he said leaning over and kissing her on the cheek.

"Okay, you go ahead Ryker, I'll meet you downstairs."

"Good," he said turning swiftly and walking out of the room.

Quickly she rose and walked cover to where her new clothes laid on the bed. She didn't have to wear a dress she thought as her hands quickly reached for an elegant ivory silk kimono sleeved duster with matching sequin embellish trimmed bustier ensemble. She put on the ensemble and stroll over to the mirror to observe her reflection. The outfit looked perfectly regal on her figure.

A half hour later, Cierra strolled into the private dining room of the White Orchid and was utterly surprised.

They were waiting for her. She froze in her tracks. Her thought was tight at the sight of her mother standing there.

Ryker stood and walked over and took her hand. "Cierra sweetness looks like my sister Isabella and my new mother-in-law have arrived."

"Cierra baby are you and Ryker married?" Ada Cantrell's voice was strained.

Cierra looked back at her mother and stammered out. "I… Ah."

Isabella blurted. "Ryker, I want to see the marriage license."

Ada's voice was gentle. "Cierra, if you and Ryker got married, I'm not angry that I didn't get to see the ceremony."

Isabella spoke up. "Hell, I for one want to see a damn marriage license."

Ryker laughed. "I knew you would Isabella," he signaled the waiter. "Perhaps we should all have a drink."

Isabella's expression was curious. "Ryker, why did you get married so quickly? And what about people who will doubt that your marriage ever happened?"

A smile tugged at the corners of Ryker's lips. "Actually, we are not married yet. We were waiting for the two of you to get here. And now that you are here, we can get started. I arranged for a room to be set up here for the nuptials. A justice of the peace is waiting. You ladies are our first-hand witnesses. This will lay to rest any doubts about our nuptials," he chuckled.

Isabella's eyes widened in complete surprise. "Ryker, I know that look, I knew you were up to something."

The waiter walked over with a tray of drinks.

Ada Cantrell wasn't a stupid woman. She heard Ryker loud and clear. Her baby Cierra wasn't married yet and in her mind, she was a mother on a mission. She held up her hand. "To hell with the drinks Ryker. Let's get this ceremony started. Where's the preacher?"

Ryker laughed. "I've arranged for a justice of the peace. He is waiting for us behind that door."

"He'll do!" Ada declared. "Come on Cierra," she said grabbing her daughter's hand.

"Ada and Cierra, hold on one moment," Isabella addressed them.

She walked over and attentively studied her brother. "Ada and Cierra, I think Ryker is up to something and I think we'd better find out what it is before this wedding takes place."

Isabella tilted her head. "Cierra, what's the definition of a taker?"

Cierra blushed. "Excuse me?"

Isabella laughed. "For heaven's sake Cierra I asked you what is a…"

Cierra interrupted. "I heard you the first time Isabella. A taker is someone who takes or seizes what they want?"

"They are masters at the game Cierra. Don't you ever forget that and my brother Ryker? Well, he is a taker. You should know this from the beginning."

Isabella adjusted Ryker's tie. "Now Brother, Ms. Ada and Cierra don't know you like I do. What are you up to?"

Ryker grinned. "Well Isabell and mother-in-law Cantrell, there is just one catch."

Ada's eyes narrowed as she looked between brother and sister.

Isabella smiled.

Ryker cleared his throat. "Well Ada and Isabella. The two of you can't tell anyone about our getting married here today."

He adjusted his tie. "And this comment is especially for you, sister. Your payment for keeping your big mouth shut is that I will graciously let you put together a small wedding at our parent's home just for the family," he paused. "And that small wedding will take place after Cierra and I come back from our honeymoon."

Isabella began to laugh helplessly. "And how long is this honeymoon?"

"You've got seven days."

Isabella placed her hands on her hips and locked eyes with her brother. "I need at least 10 days to make this wedding unforgettable."

Ryker rubbed his jaw. "Isabella we aren't negotiating."

"Yes, we are. It became a negotiation the moment I discovered what you were up to. Besides, you stole Cierra from right under my nose and just when I was about to get her married off to Dr. St. Martin's son."

"Hello you two. Cierra is a real person. She's standing here listening to the two of you negotiate her wedding."

"Oh, hush Cierra. I am so enjoying myself," Ada said, watching silently as brother and sister stared competitively at each other.

"Deal!" Ryker said finally giving in.

Ada grabbed Cierra's hand. Come on my love. It's time momma got you married."

Chapter 24

BY THE TIME TILLY LASALLE arrived at the
secluded mansion located at the top of Calaveras Road just
overlooking Calaveras reservoir, it was almost twelve
noon. She sat in her car and checked her messages. Still no
response back from her niece Cierra. She quickly dialed her
cell phone and listened as it instantly went to voice mail.
She texted her niece Cierra again.

Suddenly her car door jerked wide open.

"Damn Tilly you look amazing! What took you so
long? Get out of that car and come on inside. I'm as horny
as a dog in heat."

"Reed baby, it's so good to see you too. First give a
girl a compliment and tell her how great she looks."

Tilly LaSalle knew she looked younger than her
fifty-eight years. Her recently dyed auburn hair was

courtesy of a bottle of Revlon, and she knew the color looked good on her. She took good care of herself. She got out of the car and felt Reed run his hand down her firm, lean, well-proportioned woman's body. She made it a point to wear the empire waist dress with the heart shaped lace edging, front that showed off the swell of her breasts. Reed loved to see her in that dress.

"Oh, Tilly, you know how great you look. And that's my favorite dress." He slung an arm around Tilly's waist, he hauled her close. "Damn, I want you, I could lick you from head to toe!" he moaned.

"Hush up Reed Jefferson! Someone might hear."

"Hell woman, I live out in the middle of nowhere. My nearest neighbor is at least a mile away," Reed grinned wide, pulling her tighter into his arms.

Suddenly, without warning, Reed grabbed Tilly's ass tight and jammed his head between her heaving breasts.

Instantly Tilly felt Reed's joy greeting her.

"Ahhhh Reed darling," she said with a tilt of her head. "I can tell you're glad to see me. Come on, let's get inside."

"Damn straight woman, that's what I want to hear. My soldier has been standing at attention ever since you call."

***

An hour later, Aunt Tilly threw back her head as she sat astride of Reed raising her hips and lowering them rhythmically.

Reed was as greedy as she was she thought as she moaned as her body surged up.

All at once Reed yelled out moans of passion. He moaned wildly toward the madness of pleasure.

Minutes later she laid sprawled next to Reed on his king-sized bed.

"Damn you were incredible Tilly. Now I need a glass of aqua,"

"Put some scotch in mine," Tilly replied.

Reed walked across the room to a bar and small refrigerator. "Do you want ice or just scotch and soda?"

"No ice."

Reed brought over their drinks and sat down on the bed beside her. "What are you doing this evening?" he asked innocently.

Tilly sat up and reached for the glass he offered her. "Why? You want to play naughty girl with me later?"

"I'm always up for a game of naughty girl," Reed chuckled. "But not tonight I've got that poker game, remember? I was wondering if you wanted to go with me to Las Vegas. For the weekend?"

"Reed are you serious?" Tilly asked as her eyes lit up.

Reed grinned real wide. "Only if you want to baby. You probably won't believe this but I'm getting tired of jumping on a plane to Las Vegas and staying all by myself."

All at once Tilly grabbed his face and planted a big kiss on him. "What time does our plane leave?"

Suddenly a look of concern flashed across Reed's face. "But you know there's no sex before my poker game Tilly," he said sternly. "Oh and no sitting anywhere near my table or for that matter."

Tilly shook her head. "Reed you don't have to tell me. I know you don't want me playing poker in the same hotel that you do. You don't have to worry about me sugar."

"Good," Reed replied. "You know how serious I take my poker."

Chapter 25

THE PHONE RANGING BESIDE ENZO'S bed awoke him as he grumbled grabbing it.

"Hello."

"Hello Gigolo, did I wake you? This is Kalita baby boy, now get your ass up. We've got to go and make that money!"

"Kalita, what time is it?"

"It's get you damn ass out of the bedtime. And let's go make this fucking money!" Kalita blurted out laughing.

"Hell Kalita, I haven't had any sleep. Go spend the fucking money I made for you the last few nights," Enzo whined into the phone.

"That was just small coins compared to what I've lined up. You're not ready to quit on me already are you stud man?" She tried to sound calm, like a negotiator trying

to peek the customer's interest and finalize the deal. She
let her words sink in.

Enzo let out a big yawn. "Uh-huh, you know I enjoy
a good fuck. But a man can't live by a fuck alone. I've got
to get some sleep too," he stammered out a yawn. "How
much?"

"Big money and this gig is not just for the weekend.
This woman needs a friend and a companion for at least a
week and she's dropping down some extra cash. Now listen
up Enzo. You've got to understand that this old bitch is
really loaded."

"A week?"

Kalita let out a sigh. "I am hoping we can play this
right Enzo and we both can have a much longer stay. This
woman ain't got nobody to inherit it, if you get my
meaning?"

"What's this we stuff?"

"Oh, didn't I tell you Enzo, we've both been invited
to her Napa home."

Enzo asked. "Who is this chick anyway?"

"This ain't no chick. This is a lady and in fact she
used to be an actress. A real big famous one," Kalita
replied.

"What did you say her name was?"

"Her name is Elizabeth. Elizabeth St. John. But her
stage name was Elizabeth Starr."

Enzo's interest peaked as he sat up in bed. "The
Elizabeth Starr?"

"Yep! And she's interested in getting with you and I do mean sexually. I showed her your photo, but it was your first job for me that told her how good you were."

"What? You mean Luanne Lanchon told Elizabeth Starr about me? Well I'll be damned I'm flattered," Enzo chuckled.

They both laughed together for several moments.

And then Kalita said. "I'll pick you up in an hour. Oh, and pack enough clothes for two weeks."

Chapter 26

ELIZABETH STARR WAS THE MOST famous person Enzo Rawlins had ever met and he wondered if he looked as nervous as he felt when he was first introduced to her. He felt then like he was back in middle school trying to make the right impression on his first love. Now standing at the large oversized window looking out at the vast vineyard surrounding her Gothic Style mansion he suddenly became aware that the glass he held in his hand was empty.

The glass in his hand was his liquid courage and was now it was empty. At any minute Elizabeth Starr, the former actress, would return. He caught sight of the bar across the room and walked over to it like he owned the place and poured himself another glass of liquid courage. He threw back the glass. The scotch burned the back of his throat.

Enzo had just finished his drink when his eyes caught sight of Kalita Lopez entering the room. He poured another drink.

Kalita closed the distance between them fast and caught hold of the glass Enzo held just before he brought it to his lips. "You're not thirsty Enzo, you are just nervous."

"I am thirsty," he replied.

She took the glass out of his hands. "Stop it Enzo, you're being a fool. Look around at this grand place. Don't you like it Enzo? Don't you like being here?"

His eyes told her he did.

Kalita pressed her point. "She likes you Enzo. You made a great first impression."

Enzo grinned nervously. "I did? Did you see her? She looks like she couldn't be a day over forty. She's as sexy as hell, but I'm sure she's as old as my mother. I saw her movies as a kid. But still she's as regal as a Queen with those long legs and that buxomly chest."

"Don't doubt yourself Enzo," Kalita said casting her eyes down and admired how well he was hung. She let her hand caress across his penis. "You are the stuff women like Elizabeth dream of, strong and firm."

The corners of Enzo's lips curled into a smile. "Mmmm. I am." His mouth opened in shock. And that was the way Kalita left him.

Kalita grinned as she led him up the winding staircase, stroking his ego with her eyes with every step they took. She knew Enzo thrived on hearing how great his attributes were in bed. Kalita had figured that out about him from the moment she met him. "Even the Queen of Sheba wants a good fuck every now and then and you're excellent at doing just that Enzo," she assured him.

Enzo's chest swelled with pride as he confidently stroked his chin. "Yeah I am."

While Kalita gently encouraged Enzo, her fingers were busy removing his clothes. Before he knew it he stood in front of a double door.

"Yes, Enzo baby you are. Now you just go in there and treat Elizabeth like the Queen of Sheba and fuck the hell out of her. That's what she wants. And we both could spend the rest of our lives living here."

She removed the last of his clothes and then pushed open the bedroom door.

Naked Enzo walked into the dark bedroom with a detached smile on his face. He didn't even notice the king-sized bed was empty. He heard water splashing loudly and out of the corner of his eye he caught sight of Elizabeth stepping out of the tub. He admired her standing naked before him.

Elizabeth Starr had a toned sexual body that would put a twenty-five-year-old to shame. Her long legs and exquisite breasts were the stuff movie stars where made of.

She stood frozen to the spot, dripping wet, staring back at Enzo. As if on cue she started walking soaking wet toward the bed and laid down.

"Come Enzo," Elizabeth said calmly spreading her legs wide. "Enter me at once. "Don't worry, I don't need foreplay," she commanded.

Enzo nodded his head as if in a trance and walked toward the bed. Instantly he was on top of her and in one swift thrust he entered her, ramming her like a wild animal.

She groaned with intense pleasure and threw back her head. "Uh-huh, yes Enzo, light my fire!"

***

Over in the night, Enzo dozed lightly and turned over in his sleep. He thought he was dreaming of having gone to heaven as his ears grew attentive he heard soft moaning sounds and then felt his body's muscles tense.

He eyes flew open and he looked down.

Elizabeth, the famous movie star, was holding his erect cock in her hand licking it and giving him the best oral sex, he'd ever had. It was heavenly.

His heart hammered hard as he threw back his head and felt his climax. "Thank you, Jesus!"

"Oh no Enzo don't thank Jesus, thank Elizabeth Starr the actress who got her start doing exactly this," she giggled, licking him. "And I'm so good at it too!"

"Yes… Yes, you are!" he stammered out.

The last thing Enzo remembered was hearing Elizabeth's uncontrollable giggling and feeling the air as his body exploded in sexual ecstasy.

Chapter 27

IF THERE WAS ONE THING Isabella Leticia Granger-Duvall was good at it was putting together any event.

As far as she was concerned she was the event coordinator extraordinaire, director, planner and any other title she could give herself. But putting together a wedding in seven days at her parents' home and keeping them from knowing what she was doing was pure hell she thought, as she checked over the guest list again. Every person on the guest list had loose lips as far as she was concerned, and loose lips sank more ships than she'd ever care to remember. How can I hold a wedding and not let on that it is a wedding?

Instantly the answer was obvious. She would announce it not as a wedding but as a surprise party. She dialed Ada Cantrell's number.

The phone rang once before it was picked up.

"Hello Ada, it's me Isabella," she said but didn't wait for a response. "Are you free today?"

"Yes of course I am," Ada replied. "I can tell by your voice you've got an idea."

"Yes, I do but I need your help."

Ada's voice was calm. "I'm listening."

"Well Ada, how would you like to spend some time cruising around Carmel, Pismo Beach and maybe even San Simeon?"

"Is there something going on, maybe some type of festival?"

"Well for starters there's the Clam Bake Festival in Pismo Beach."

"Keep talking, I'm listening," Ada said.

"Well, I've just come up with the perfect idea to get my folks out of the house for a few days. But I need your help?"

Ada laughed. "Okay."

"Can you come over for lunch at my parents' home today?"

"Sure, if you think I could help."

"Yes, you can. You see my parents love to travel in their RV and they have a buddy named Kirkland Jones. He and my father both love to travel in that big old RV of his. Only, my mother gets a little lonely with the two guys talking about guy things all the time. Usually I go alone with them to keep her company," Isabella quickly explained her idea. "Your being there will keep my mother occupied and allow me to set up their home for the wedding. I promised Ryker I'd keep it secret."

***

Several hours later Ada hummed softly as she got out of Isabella's Mercedes. It was a beautiful day and it called up a song from her memory. She cleared her throat. "I hope your parents don't mind my tagging along," she said.

"Trust me, they will enjoy the company. Besides, I've already told you my mother enjoys your company," Isabella replied emerging from her car and popping the trunk. She immediately glanced at the RV parked in the driveway and saw the man stepping up into it. She quickly stole a look back at Ada. She hadn't noticed a thing.

"Ada, I want to run in the house for a moment. Can I ask a favor, and have you take your overnight bag to the RV for me?" Isabella asked waving her hand in the direction of the RV.

"Sure, I can do that," Ada noted, watching Isabella heading inside. She started humming "you're beautiful" again. The song was her favorite. She started humming the song out loud.

Ada turned her attention to the RV and quickly walked over to where it was parked.

Nearing the RV, she noticed the steps leading to door. She went to step up when the door swung open.

A man opened the door wide. He wore a short-sleeved denim shirt and jeans. He didn't look happy. "Who are you?"

Ada felt her heart pounding in her chest.

"I'm Ada Cantrell. I'm a friend of the Grangers."

"Hmm," the man said as his lips tightened. "Here, let me take that bag for you Ada. I see you're a hummer," he softly smiled. "I'm partial to humming myself. By the way I'm Tucker Justice Jones but my friends, Colbert and Lana Granger, call me Tuck. So, since you are going to be going with us to the Clam Festival I guess its okay if you call me Tuck too."

The two of them stood there staring at each other.

Someone touched Ada's shoulder from behind. "Hey Ada, I see you've met Tuck."

She turned around. "Hi Lana, yes and Tuck and I were just getting acquainted."

Lana laughed. "Good, I for one am ready to hit the road."

Ada glanced back at the house. "Where's Isabella?"

"Oh, my little assistant persuaded me to let her lock up the house," Lana said with a nod. "Knowing Isabella, she's probably going to spend the night," she said walking over to the table area of the RV.

At that moment her husband Colbert boarded the RV, with the chauffeur, Rex. "Hello everyone. This is Rex.

He's going to be doing the driving. It seems my doctor won't allow me to do any driving. But that's okay with Rex driving, we can make it to Pismo Beach before the sunsets and I've got my mouth all set to have a bowl of their famous clam chowder when we get there."

"Hmmm that sounds good," Lana said nodding. "But right now, I want to play some cut-throat Jamaican Dominoes. Ada, want to play?"

"That sounds like fun!" Ada replied, joining her at the table.

"If Ada's playing I want to play," Tuck said sulkily leaning over and whispering to Colbert.

Colbert rolled his eyes as their chauffeur Rex started up the RV's engine. "Ah I guess that means I have to play too. Oh well, I knew once Ada agreed to go along on this trip you'd agree to do whatever the ladies wanted," he chuckled.

***

Hours later Colbert had suggested they all walk Pismo Beach Pier and walk off the delicious bowls of clam chowder they'd enjoyed. He and Lana had managed to make sure Tuck and Ada were alone together at every opportunity.

The view along the pier was euphoric. Ada thought with a long sigh as she stood there taking it all in.

Tuck eyed her appraisingly. Then grinned and rubbed his chin. "You look amazing. I mean after you beat me at dominoes I was determined to not like you," he grinned. "You hurt my pride," he jokingly said, as he reached out to touch her hand.

Ada felt desire shoot through her like lightning. Tuck was a man who liked to touch and each time he did it made her warm inside. "I didn't mean to. In fact, having you sitting so close to me was almost a distraction.

Tuck's good looks alone had made him different from many men. But his quiet honest nature seemed to draw Ada like a moth to a flame.

"I liked sitting next to you. In fact, since we are all alone I hope you don't mind if I do this," Tuck said, leaning over as his mouth claimed hers, softly and gently.

It was a full thirty seconds before Ada pulled out of his embrace. "I hope you know Tuck; I don't go around just kissing men."

"You didn't. I kissed you. Sorry, but I couldn't resist," he replied.

Giggling slightly, she replied. "Yes, I guess you did," she hesitated. "And I have to say, I enjoyed it.

All at once Ada's cell phone rang. She retrieved her phone and said. "I have to take this. It's from my sister Tilly. I haven't heard from her all day."

"No Problem," Tuck said, taking a step away.

"Hello Tilly, where have you been?"

"Oh, thank God I reached you Ada. I just called to let you know not to expect me at home for a few days. I'm in Las Vegas with a friend," Tilly replied.

"Las Vegas? Tilly you're not there playing poker?" Ada asked.

Tilly breathed out. "Stop worrying Ada. I'm here with Reed Jefferson. You know the Reed, the one with the large bank account?"

"Whatever Tilly. Just don't you be playing cards with any of your own money?" Ada scolded.

Tilly changed the subject. "How's Cierra? Has she made any progress dating those two, what's their names?"

Ada didn't want to talk about family business especially when standing not far from her was a single, available, handsome man. "Look Tilly, Cierra's okay, but I really can't talk right now."

"Sounds like you're on a date?" Tilly inquired.

"Yeah, sort of," Ada said, sounding like a teenager.

"Well, thank God for that. I guess miracles do happen. Well sister, we'll talk later. I don't want to hold up your date," Tilly paused. "Oh and do have a good time Ada. You go out so seldom that you deserve to enjoy yourself."

Ada shook her head grinning. "Okay, I'll talk with you soon. Bye."

Right after she ended her call Lana and Colbert joined them.

"I'm ready to turn in," Colbert said. "That long drive and the walk on the beach has made me sleepy. By the way, I booked us a couple rooms at the Cliff House Resort."

Lana joined in the conversation. "So, you got a couple of rooms. Does that mean the men will bunk together? And the women will bunk together?"

Colbert chuckled out. "Fat chance wife, we've never slept apart. Besides, I thought you love to listen to me snore?"

Lana moved in closer and leaned over and whispered at Ada. "Ada, if you don't feel comfortable sharing a room with Tuck I understand. But just so you know I checked, and the room has double beds. You know always means a woman has a chance at a good night's sleep."

Ada threw back her head, her laughter filling the air delightfully as her eyes sparkled mischievously. "Double beds, really? Who said I wanted a good night's sleep."

Chapter 28

ENZO COULD NOT BELIEVE HIS LUCK when he opened his eyes lying in bed. Across the room, perched in a chair sipping a mug of coffee and reading a magazine sat Elizabeth Starr, the famous actress.

"Good morning," Enzo murmured. "I thought I was dreaming."

"God no Enzo, you weren't dreaming that was me fucking your brains out last night darling," she said seriously. "Would you like a cup of coffee? The house is always chilly this time of the morning."

She poured him a mug of coffee and then wafted over to the bed, like she was in a scene from a movie and sat down beside him.

"Enzo darling, I know you like Elizabeth Starr the actress, but Elizabeth St. John the person is in a big of a jam," she said in a soft voice.

Enzo laughed and took the mug of coffee from her hand. "You sound serious. What is it?"

She let out a nervous sigh. "I feel like such a fool for asking you this, but today I need you to pretend like we've been lovers for a long time"

"Is that all? I think I can manage that."

Elizabeth managed a slight smile. For a brief moment she relaxed. "I am afraid you don't understand. A friend of mine is expecting to see me and my new...Ah friend today."

"Oh really?" Enzo replied, acting like it was no big deal.

"Yes, we are expected at a late lunch this afternoon. From there we head off to a party. This is serious. You've got to put on the performance of your life," she stated with a slight edge of panic in her voice.

Enzo saluted her. "Yes Capitan, I think I can manage that."

"Okay then my handsome young soldier, now we are on the same page. So, how's your French?" she asked with a nervous edge.

He grinned. "I took Spanish in high school. This is California you know?"

"I thought as much," she frowned. "Well I'm giving you a crash course. The only words I want pouring off those sexy lips of yours today is "Mon L'amoure! Or maybe Oui! Oui!"

Enzo lifted his eyes and stared disbelieving into hers. "Are you kidding me?"

Elizabeth stared back at him as if preoccupied with her own fears. Suddenly she rose off of the bed and stood there a moment staring down at him. She pulled on a robe and walked to the door. "Look Enzo, this isn't a game," she opened the door.

"Kalita you said Enzo was trainable. I'm sorry, but I don't see that," Elizabeth retorted angrily.

Kalita Lopez walked in. "Don't worry Elizabeth I will take care of this," she commanded.

She walked over and gave Enzo her full attention. She took the mug of coffee from his hands. "Enzo darling. Elizabeth is not kidding," she sneered. "Elizabeth is paying good money for you to act the part she needs you to act. Now I need you to get out of bed. Get showered and dressed. And put on that Armani suit that is hanging in the closet for you to wear."

"Christ, you're serious?" Enzo declared as he blinked staring between Elizabeth and Kalita. At that moment he realized what it meant to see yourself as valueless in the eyes of another person. He wondered if this was how a prostitute felt when she sold her body for the pleasure of another person.

As of on clue Elizabeth stepped across the threshold of the door. She paused and looked back at him. "Oh, and Enzo if you must call my name today. Please refer to me as your Imperial Royal Highness Elizabeth Starr," she gave a wicked giggle and made her exit.

Chapter 29

LATER THAT EVENING, OUT OF THE CORNER of his eyes Enzo watched Kalita steer in his direction.

"Don't look so sad Enzo. This dinner party is over and everyone's leaving," Kalita said sweetly as she halted in front of him. "By the way, the divine Imperial Royal Highness is very happy with your performance today. Want to see how much?" She asked placing a slip of paper in his hand.

"What is this?" Enzo asked before opening the slip of paper in his hand. He whistled out in surprised delight. "When did you deposit this in my bank account?"

Kalita shrugged. "I slipped off before we arrived for dinner."

Enzo was stunned by the large amount. "I didn't expect…"

"Don't be ridiculous Enzo, you deserve every dollar. Like I told you before her royal highness is paying you very well to be her special friend."

"Well thanks Kalita. I didn't expect to see the fruits of my labor to be so productive so soon," he chuckled jokingly.

"Don't thank me so soon", Kalita warned. "Come on let's get out of here. Her royal highness arranged for a limousine to take us back to her house. Here, share the last of this wine with me before we leave."

Enzo heard the edge in her voice and regarded her with a long measuring gaze. He took the glass of wine. "I take it this glass of wine is special."

"Yeah, consider it my concoction of happy juice. It's spiked, just so you know," Kalita said as her eyes darted across the room. "You see that tan young blond with the sad dark eyes standing by the staircase?"

Enzo's eyes followed hers. Just at that moment he saw the girl hurry up the staircase. "Yeah, sure I see her."

"That's the divine Imperial royal highness' pleasure for the evening," Kalita took the glass from his hand and finished it. "And she wants her dessert served up with you fucking her brains out"

"You sound a little jealous," Enzo nodded.

"Me jealous? I don't know the meaning of the word," Kalita replied.

"So, when is this supposed to take place?"

"Why do you think we're heading back to her place right now?" Kalita asked but didn't wait for his response.

She put down the empty wine glass and laced her arms in his. "Come on stud man, I've got to get you bathed and ready for your royal highness. The limo is waiting."

**

An hour later Enzo emerged from the shower. He stood still while Kalita rubbed his body with the oil that aroused his sensual senses.

"Mmmm, that smell is intoxicating. What is it?" he curiously asked.

"That smell is a secret aphrodisiacs oil mixture that I've concocted myself. By the way what I'm doing is stimulating the largest sensory organ on your body, your skin," she replied.

Enzo regarded her with watchful eyes. "You know Kalita, you remind me of a coach with a hands-on approach. I like that way you always get your fighter ready to do battle."

He looked back at her and smiled. "Thanks coach," he grabbed her and hugged her tight. "I think all that money you deposited into my bank account made me feel like I can trust you."

Kalita was momentarily confused as she felt something deep inside. Cautiously she pulled out of his embrace. "Hold up. Wait a minute stud man. What's the big idea? Don't go forgetting this is business. You're my investment. I've got a duty to look out for you."

She looked longingly back at him. His smile reminded her of a boy she once knew a long time ago. Back when she was growing up in the small town of Dos Palos California. He was the only person she could trust. They were both from single parent households. They were both poor. She stared back at him a second to linger and remember the boy. At the end of the day she was still human. What did she have to lose? She reached up and softly kissed him on the lips. "Come on stud man you've got a performance to do."

Chapter 30

Moon, Stars, Ada

ADA TRIED NOT TO STARE AS SHE
WATCHED Lana and Colbert Granger kissing like high
school kids in front of her.

"You'd better get used to seeing what Lana and
Colbert are always doing. You'd think the two of them
would have gotten it out of their system after being married
for so long," Tucker noted with a husky laugh.

"Tucker Justice Jones you need to handle your
business and tell Ada you're just a little bit in love with her
yourself," Colbert blabbed out.

Tucker sucked in a deep breath startled by his
friend's revelation. "Ah Colbert old buddy."

"Colbert! Lana exclaimed. "You shouldn't spread
Tuck's business like that. If you do, then you should tell the
whole truth. This isn't the first time Tucker has met Ada,"

she shook her head. "Aren't I right Tucker? You've seen her before."

Ada stared back at Tucker in shock. She didn't believe what she had heard. "You have," she stammered. "I mean this isn't the first time we've met?"

"No, it isn't," Tucker replied.

Lana grabbed Colbert by the hand. "Come on blabber mouth. This sounds like a private conversation. Let's give Tuck and Ada their space," she said pulling him out of distance.

Tucker waited until they were out of hearing distance. "Ada, I can't believe you don't remember we danced at the Halloween Mask Ball."

All at once Ada chuckled. "You were the guy dressed in the mummy costume. The one who got mad when Reed Jefferson walked past and slap me on the butt?"

"Yep, I'm the one. Colbert taped my mouth shut that night. I got angry when I saw Reed with you earlier," Tucker explained. "Colbert told me I would be more mysterious to you if I didn't talk. So, I let him wrap more bandages around my mouth. He taped my mouth good and shut. I think he really did that because he knew I wanted to give Reed a piece of my mind for dancing with you, all close and stuff, earlier. The only thing it really accomplished was keeping me from telling you my name or giving you my telephone number."

Ada shook her head. "Now I remember. I wore that stupid genie costume. It came complete with a blonde ponytail wig and a veil that covered my face. The funny thing is it was supposed to have been my sister Tilly's

costume. I was supposed to wear a Greek Goddess
costume but Tilly thought it looked better on her. Reed
thought that I was Tilly. Because she told him that she was
wearing the genie costume. Besides Reed was drunk from
the minute he knock on the door," she said.

"Yeah, Colbert told me as much. But it still made
me want to punch the guy," he replied.

"Reeds a good guy and I'm pretty sure he's in love
with my sister Tilly, but neither one of them is willing to let
down their pride enough to find that out."

They chatted for more than an hour.

Ada leaned over the rail and gazed out at the ocean.
The moon, stars and ocean made the night a romantic,
beautiful scene. It also made her think about the big secret
she had sworn not to tell. Besides that, Ryker and Cierra
looking so happy together made her realize that there was
more in her life now. She no longer had to stay focused on
her daughter. She glanced back at Tucker for a moment and
she remembered back to that faithful day she'd seen him
and thought he was attractive. The first time she saw him
was many months ago at the Grangers Annual Memorial
Day Barbeque. Tucker wore a white t-shirt and jeans. He
was helping Colbert at the grill. She remembered how
ripped and muscular his arms looked against the white t-
shirt he'd worn. He had the muscles and body of a man
who kept himself in shape. She liked that. "Do you want to
know what kind of guys I'm attracted too Tucker?" she
asked but didn't wait for an answer. "I'm attracted to guys
like you. By the way I've noticed you before too."

Tucker breathed out a sigh of relief. "Are you serious? When?"

She nodded. "We've move around in the same social circle for a while now. And I've seen you a few places before. But I think the first time you really caught my eye was back at the Granger's Annual Memorial Day Barbeque," she said. "You were wearing one of those t-shirts that showed off your muscles. God, I thought you looked magnificent barbequing that meat on the grill. You were the handsomest master chef I've ever seen!"

There was a flash of remembrance in his eyes. Leaning in closer, Tucker's face lite up into a smile. "You thought I looked handsome and magnificent?" He grinned.

Ada thoughts raced. She didn't want him to know she'd had a crush on him from that moment on. She'd even asked her sister Tilly about him and was amazed when Tilly had told her she had heard that Tucker was a fantastic lover.

She let out a low throaty chuckle. "I forgot men love compliments just as much as women do."

"Yeah we do," Tucker excitedly blurted out with laughter.

Ada smiled. "You have a fantastic laugh. It fits your personality." She sucked in a deep breath remembering she hadn't had sex in a long time. She stared hard at him.

"What are you thinking?" Tucker asked.

"I was just hoping I wasn't boring you. What were you thinking about?" she asked a wry smile playing on her lips.

A grin played on his lips. "You couldn't bore me if you tried," he reached for her.

She let him pull her into his embrace. She felt like she had forgotten how to breathe. "Tucker you feel so good," she said wrapping her arms around him.

He was encouraged by her swift response to him. "I'm a happy man right now. Holding you feels so wonderful. But I'm still a man and if I don't let you go real soon I'd better become a man with a truck load of self-control. You are lethal woman."

Ada gave a small sigh. "You should know I'm a sucker for a compliment," her thoughts raced, as she said inside her mind. "*And I haven't been with a man in a long time. I just might be in the mood to give a man with limited self-control a lot of mercy.*"

Startled by her thoughts she leaned back and said. "Goodness, I wish I knew what you were thinking right now."

He leaned back and studied her face. "Do you really want to know what I was thinking?" he asked with a sigh of anticipation as he leaned in close. "I was thinking that I wished you would consider going someplace we can be alone."

Ada's eyes danced with excitement. "I was thinking the same thing too. In fact, I was thinking that I was in a good mood to give a lucky man like you a lot of tender mercy. If you know what I mean?"

"Then woman, please have mercy on me," Tucker said as he took her face in his hands and drew her near and kissed her softly.

Suddenly he pulled her close again, his lips pressing hard against hers. Passion ignited as his mouth captured hers hungrily. He pulled away. "I do have a hotel room all to myself for the night."

"What, you're not sleeping in the RV?" she jokingly asked.

"No, and neither are you?"

Chapter 31

AT FOUR O'CLOCK THAT MORNING, ISABELLA and Stuart Duvall were awaken by the ferocious ringing of their front doorbell.

Stuart Duvall, ever protective of his wife Isabella, stumbled out of bed and belted his robe and headed for the front door.

"Who is it?" Stuart yelled yanking open the front door.

"Desiree... Desiree Martin!"

He stared at her.

"Hi Stuart, I know it's awfully late, but I just have to talk to Isabella."

Stuart didn't care what the reason was for Desiree's visit. He was just relieved that his wife Isabella was right behind him.

"Isabella, it's for you. Do you want me to leave you alone with her?"

"Yeah, go on back to bed Stuart. I can handle this," Isabella said as she shook her head. "Come on in Desiree and this had better be good."

Desiree was all jitters. She held up her hand. "Oh Isabella, could you make me a cup of your fabulous instant coffee?"

"Okay, instant it is. But tea not coffee. I'm not too sure about the fabulous part. Come on into the kitchen.

Desiree walked over to the table and started to sit down.

"Don't sit in that chair, Desiree. One of Stuart's friends broke it and I haven't had a chance to have it repaired."

Isabella busied herself putting the kettle on the stove. "I'll get the hot water started," she announced filling the kettle with water and placing it on the stove.

She walked over and sat down across from Desiree. "Okay Desiree, what's happening with you?"

Like an actress rehearsing a roll. She lowered her head sadly and lifted it as her face contorted through several expressions. "I... I don't know what to think," she paused as her lips curled into a frown. "I heard Ryker got himself married to some girl named Cierra Cantrell."

Shocked with disbelief Isabella stared at her. "Who? What? Where did you hear that?"

Desiree gave a crisp laugh. "Ah huh! Then it is true. I can tell by that look on your face."

Isabella sat back in her chair and looked at the woman she once called friend, sitting across from her.

"I don't understand Desiree. Who told you?"

"Let's just say a little bird. And I didn't believe it at first. But once I saw that look on your face I knew it was true."

At that moment Isabella knew she was sitting next to pure malice. "So, if that's all you wanted to know…"

"But that's not why I'm here," Desiree interrupted. "You do remember that I tried to get you to tell your brother Ryker I was still seeing Marquise?"

Isabella fought to control her temper. "Yes, but you know I wasn't about to get involved in your business with Ryker," she said with loathing.

"Well you should have told him. Then maybe your brother would have stopped dropping by to dip his penis in my business. You know how much Ryker loves having sex," her voice tinkled with laughter.

"Why are you telling me this Desiree?"

"Because I'm going to have Ryker's baby and the worst part about all of this is that the whore of a wife he married is going to have his Brother Steele's child. Or didn't Cierra tell you she had slept with your brother Steele?"

Isabella's mouth opened in shocked. She collected her thoughts and studied Desiree. She kept her cool and took a deep breath. "Quite a performance Desiree. Would you like for me to offer you a little advice?" She asked but didn't wait for a response. "The next time you tell that story you should show a little emotion and whip up a tear or two. Anyway, I'll show you to the guest room. You can spend the night."

"What?" Desiree asked innocently.

Isabella gave her a sly smile. "Did you think for one moment that I was just going to pick up the phone and call Ryker and tell him what you just said?"

"Well...I...

"You thought wrong," Isabella said in a mulish voice.

Desiree stared at her astounded. "Why Isabella, married life is making you grown and mean with horns."

"And being single and stupid after thirty-five is making you a nasty piece of rag," Isabella said in a harsh tone.

"Isabella you know I've just turned thirty. Now take that back or else!"

"Or else what?" Isabella interrupted, a tad sarcastic. "You'll hold your breath until you pass out?"

"You'd be sorry if I did," Desiree said with conviction. "I can see it now, I'll fall over and hurt myself. Maybe even miscarry or something."

"Oh, cut the crap Desiree and shut up. Before you lose a warm and free bed to sleep in for the night."

All at once the tea kettle whistled loudly.

A frown crossed Isabella's face as she walked over and turned off the stove and removed the kettle. "Get on your feet Desiree I'll show you to your room."

"Isabella aren't you going to make your guest a cup of tea first."

"Hell no!"

Chapter 32

"STUD MAN, WHAT ARE YOU DOING DRESSED and out of bed?" Kalita asked.

"Dawn has arisen over the horizon and I saw the light of a new day. I think I read that in a book," Enzo stated as if reciting a line in a play," he thrust his hands into his pockets. "No seriously, I've been waiting on you to wake up. I'm out of here."

Kalita's face went stone dead. "What?"

"Oh yeah, did I mention that that wicked creature known as the Imperial Royal Highness better known as the actress Elizabeth Starr said that she no longer needs my services. She has found herself a new toy with that overly tan young blond with the sad dark eyes. Who, by the way, is a hermaphrodite?"

Kalita flinched. "The correct term is intersex."

"Whatever Kalita. I still don't have a clue. Anyway, I started to act like I was put out about it when I found out that it was intersex, but your Imperial Royal Highness gave me a nice fat check to keep on screwing the two of them. Which by the way, I ain't sharing a dime of it with you?"

Kalita chuckled, noticing how much Enzo sounded like a little kid. "No problem. So where are you on your way to, may I ask?"

"I'm off to Las Vegas to spend some my new-found wealth on filling my head with some good memories."

"Can I come too?" Kalita asked in a soft voice. "I promise to help you make some good memories. Don't worry, I have my own money. Remember, I'm an independent woman."

Chapter 33

AT NINE O'CLOCK THE NEXT MORNING
Isabella felt she'd let Desiree sleep long enough. She stood
outside the guest room and rapped on the door four times.

"No answer."

"Desiree… Desiree... Are you dressed yet?" she
called as she entered the well decorated room.

A frown crossed Isabella's face. Desiree wasn't in
the room. And then she heard the shower running. Desiree
was in the shower.

She walked over to an ornate sculpture standing in
the corner and pressed the secret compartment. The hidden
video surveillance system was still working.

She turned and retraced her steps back out the
bedroom and walked silently down the hall. Walking
toward the stairs she thought she saw a figure walk around

the curve of the stairway and head into the room that was her office.

"That's impossible," she mumbled under her breath. "I just left Desiree in the shower."

Isabella leaned in close flush against the wall and tiptoed down the hall. She stood outside the door. She listened as Desiree punched numbers into her cell phone.

"Hello lover, it's me Desiree," she whispered into the phone. "Sorry I can't talk any louder. Guess what I dug up?"

Desiree paused for a moment listening. "Look, you'll never guess, so I'll tell you," she said into the phone. "Isabella is putting together a wedding here for Ryker and Cierra, at their family home."

"What? Of course, I know what I'm talking about. I'm not making this stuff up!" Desiree yelled into the phone.

Whoever Desiree was talking to on the phone needed convincing.

She breathed out. "Of course, I'm sure. I'm looking at the guest list and the list of arrangements Isabella has already made. She's planning a wedding."

Isabella listened as Desiree and the person she was speaking to shoot back profanities.

Desiree seemed to let the person she was speaking to have a long rant.

Finally, all at once Desiree said. "Look here lover. This girl must make a living. So, I'm going to tell you what we are going to do. We are going to let this wedding take place and then we're going to crash it," she blurted. "You need to count your lucky stars that I'm helping you. I'll call you as soon as I get away from here," she paused. "Anyway, I need to get back to my room. Isabella still thinks I'm having a long shower. I've got to go," she said abruptly hanging up.

Silently easing back down the hallway. Isabella reflected on just what she overheard. Who was the man or woman that Desiree was talking to at the other end of the phone? Isabella made up her mind it had to be a man. The only question was who the man was.

She walked toward the kitchen determined to make herself a pot of coffee.

***

An hour later, Isabella played innocent as she watched Desiree finish the breakfast that she'd made.

"Hmm, this coffee is so good. You see Isabella, I only said all those stupid things last night because I was starving."

"You expect me to believe that lame excuse? Desiree you made a serious allegation."

Desiree shook her head. "Oh, stop *trippin* Isabella. You know I'm crazy and I don't respect other people. Look, I'm sorry for saying all those mean things last night. I was hurt and angry."

Isabella looked back at her. She stopped short of saying what she really wanted to say.

"You don't have to a say a word. I know you agree with me. And one of these days Isabella," she said with a resigned shrug. "I'm going to grow up and start respecting other people and treating them right."

Isabella stared at Desiree with a moment of cold silence until finally Desiree broke the ice.

"Ah, look at the time," Desiree said, reaching for her purse. "I really need to get home and change. The only thing I brought with me last night was my purse. I know you've been wanting me to leave so I'm going to get going. Forget about everything I said last night."

Desiree headed for the door.

Isabella followed close behind. She walked to the driveway and watched Desiree get into her car and drive away.

"You lying bitch!" Isabella blurted, under her breath, as she watched Desiree's car drive away.

Chapter 34

ISABELLA PACED HER OFFICE trying to think of what to do. Finally, she reached for the phone and dialed the number.

It picked up after the first ring.

"Hello Ryker, it's me Isabella."

"Oh, it must be important," he said.

"Yes, it is. We have a problem. I think we need to change the location of the wedding."

Quickly Isabella filled Ryker in on what had happened the night before and that morning.

Finally, she said. "I wish I knew who she was talking to."

"Did you say anything to Desiree about knowing what you overheard?" he asked.

"No Ryker, or she never would have left this morning so easily. I don't think Desiree suspects a thing," she cleared her throat. "Ryker, what about what she said about Cierra sleeping with Steele?"

"What do you think Isabella?"

Isabella thought about it for a moment. "I think it was a lie. In fact, I'm sure Desiree said that to get a rise out of me. Cierra isn't that type of girl."

"On that sister, we agree. Cierra isn't the type that would do something like that. Besides, I've learned something after losing Indira. I not about to let someone I love become a victim like Indira Jones was set up to be."

"That's good to hear brother," Isabella said, taking a deep breath. In the next breath, she said. "If you don't mind brother, I think we should move this wedding location and date."

She quickly filled him in on the details.

"Do you think you can do that Isabella? I get our parents to agree to meet in Las Vegas?"

She laughed. "You leave everything to me, my big brother."

***

Later in the day, Isabella called Ada Cantrell and told her there was a change in plans.

"So, there it is Ada. The wedding plans have changed. Everyone is going to meet in Las Vegas."

Ada sounded upbeat. "Isabella are you sure you've got everything under control? Are you sure you don't want me to say anything to your mother?"

Isabella's tone was firm. "Oh no, I don't want her to get any story, but the one I'm going to give. Just wait until my mother tells you that they are driving over to Las Vegas."

"Very well, I'll wait to have Lana tell me about the change in plans."

***

Isabella hung up the phone and quickly dialed her mother's number.

Lana answered on the first ring.

"Isabella, what's wrong darling?"

"Mother are you alone? Can you talk privately?"

"Sure darling. You sound distressed. What's wrong?"

Isabella said a short prayer and told her mother the truth. Quickly, she filled her in on a few of the details about Desiree's cheap theatrics designed to crash the wedding she ruin the wedding that she had planned. She made it a point to leave out a few details.

Lana's voice was excited. "I can't believe it. My son Ryker is finally getting married!"

"So, you see mother, I need to move Ryker's and Cierra's wedding to Las Vegas. Do you think you can get daddy to take you there? Pismo Beach is just down the road."

"And how daughter, you don't even have to worry. We'll all be there with bells on."

"Oh, and Mom. You can't tell a soul about Ryker's and Cierra's wedding," Isabella hesitated for a second. "And for Christ's sake, don't tell Ada.

"Seriously?"

"Yes mother, I'm serious," Isabella answered instantly. "Cierra wants her mother to be surprised. And we want Cierra to be happy, right?"

"Oh, yes," Lana replied.

Isabella kept her voice smooth and cool. "You know mother that there is a great satisfaction in knowing something that others don't know about."

"Yes, Isabella I agree," Lana said. "Especially when that something brings happiness to so many people."

Chapter 35

HIS MUFFLED VOICE SOUNDED THROUGH the bathroom door.

"Ada why are you hiding in the bathroom?"

"I was taking a private call Tucker and I didn't want to wake you," she smiled as she walked out and sat on the side of the bed. She placed her cell phone on the table.

"I woke up the moment I felt you wiggling beneath me. Now woman, why are you talking private calls and hiding in the bathroom from me? Are you ashamed of being with me? Having sex, I mean."

"Oh, for God's sake," she responded.

"I get it," Tucker argued. "You don't want our friends to know we've been doing the sex thing, right?"

She scowled at his perception. "I'm not one for broadcasting my business to everyone. I have a daughter you know."

Just as the word rolled off her tongue Ada's cell phone rang.

She looked up in apprehension and reached for her phone on the side of the bed. "Tucker it's my daughter, Cierra I have to take this. And for your information. She was the one I was on the phone with earlier," she lied.

Tucker touched his finger to her lips and whispered. "Tell her I said hi," he said, rising from the bed and heading for the bathroom.

Ada cleared her throat. "Hello Cierra baby is everything alright?"

"Mom, where are you?" Cierra asked.

Ada paused to think before she answered. "Oh, I'm not too far away from home," she lied, realizing this was the second lie she'd just told that morning.

"Oh really. Anyway, that's not why I called you. Mom do you know where your sister is?"

"Your Aunt Tilly is probably just getting home at this time of the morning."

"No, she's not. She called me, and I think she's in Las Vegas," Cierra replied.

"Las Vegas! With her gambling habit?" Ada screeched.

"Mom calm down. Don't worry. She called me because she can't reach you."

Ada sucked in her breath. "Well, if she thinks I'm sending her money."

"No mom, Aunt Tilly went to Las Vegas with Reed Jefferson. She just wants you to give her a call."

"Where is she staying in Las Vegas?"

"She's staying at the Venetian Hotel under Reed Jefferson's name. She should still be in the room right now.

I just got off the phone and promised her I'd try to reach you."

"Urgent! What does Tilly call urgent?"

"Mom just call her and find out and stop worrying. Oh, and call me back if it is something serious."

"Okay," Ada said hanging up the phone and took a deep breath and dialed her sister's cell phone number.

The phone picked up on the second ring.

"Hello Tilly? It's me Ada. Cierra tells me you were looking for me."

"Oh sister! Reed Jefferson asked me to marry him. You've got to come to Vegas this instant. I won't get married unless you're here."

For once in her life Ada was speechless. She glanced back at the bathroom door and made sure it was closed. With a trembling voice she said. "Tilly, I don't believe it," she cleared her throat. "I didn't mean it like that Tilly. It's just...Tilly are you sure you want to do this? I mean get married and all?"

"What do you mean am I sure? Of course, I'm sure. Reed asked me, and I said yes. And he is willing to wait until you get her before we get married. Now, how soon can you get a flight to Las Vegas?"

Ada walked across the room and stared out of the window. Her voice was anxious. "Well, I don't know. Right now, I'm traveling with a few friends."

"Don't pretend I don't know who you're with Ada. You are my sister you know," Tilly laughed out. "Besides, I overheard you on the telephone with Lana talking about taking some trip to Pismo Beach. That was Lana Granger you were talking too, right?"

"Yeah…But!"

Tilly interrupted. "I'm guessing Colbert drove that RV of his," Tilly told her. "Say why don't you invite them to come to Las Vegas with you?"

"I don't know Tilly."

"Come on Ada, you know Reed and Colbert go way back. Besides, it's only a few hours ride from Pismo Beach. I'm sure Colbert would love to make the drive. Please Ada," she pleaded

"Oh, Tilly alright. I'm not promising you, but I'll talk to Lana and Colbert Granger," Ada said leaving out Tucker's name. "And if they are okay with it, I'll call you and confirm we are on our way."

"That sounds like a plan. I know you can swing it. I love you Ada girl!"

Ada hung up the phone with a heavy sigh. As if her life wasn't complicated enough.

"What's wrong sweetheart?" Tucker asked, as he walked back into the room.

Ada furrowed her brows. "That was my sister Tilly on the phone. She's getting married!"

"To Reed Jefferson I presume?

"Yes, and in Las Vegas! And she expects me to persuade Lana and Colbert to go to Vegas and see her get married."

Tucker closed the distance between them. "Oh, what about me? Your sister's invitation didn't include me?"

"Oh, Tucker darling, can't you see I can't believe all of this is happening."

Tucker chuckled softly. "Ada darling, that's why you've got me. I'm the man who will help you uncomplicate this whole mess."

Chapter 36

DESIREE MARTIN HAD ALWAYS THOUGHT that the Granger home, sitting on the top of Sunset Mountain, was her dream home. She'd always envisioned herself living there.

Standing there looking around the empty driveway and backyard she felt sick.

A man's angry voice sliced the air. "Where is everyone Desiree? You told me there was supposed to be a wedding here today."

"Steele there was supposed to be," she said in a panicked voice. "I … I."

Steeled turned and gave her a scolding look of contempt. "I don't see a wedding Desiree. Do you see a wedding?"

A car drove down the hill.

Desiree froze. "Look, that's Emma Calumet. The Granger's neighbor. "Maybe she knows what happened to the wedding today," she said, getting out of the SUV and flagging down the car.

Steele immediately followed behind her.

The car slowly pulled over.

The late model black Mercedes Benz coach model reminded Desiree of a hearse.

The car window rolled down.

"Hello Mrs. Calumet. Remember me?" Desiree called out not wanting to creep closer to the car.

"Yes, I remember you Desiree. You're Isabella's friend. My goodness you're dressed fancy today. What's the occasion?"

"I thought today there was supposed to be a wedding here," Desiree said.

"Why did you think that?" Mrs. Calumet asked but didn't wait for a reply. "Can't you see the house is empty? Besides, didn't you read Silicon Valley Eastside Gossip Column?"

"What?" Steele and Desiree said in Unisom.

Mrs. Calumet reached for the newspaper lying on the empty car seat next to her. "It states right here that Ryker Lamont Granger is to marry a Miss Cierra Lillianna Cantrell, in Las Vega Nevada at that Rose Chapel, today."

"What the hell!"

Before the words left her mouth, Desiree looked up just as Steele's SUV took off down the road.

"Steele!" she yelled after him.

Chapter 37

THE RV WAS PARKED IN THE RV PARKING LOT, just down the street from the Venetian Hotel.

It was the perfect day for a wedding, Tucker thought as he nudged Ada. "Ada darling wake up."

"What's wrong Tucker?"

"Nothing I just thought you might want to go back inside. Before someone misses us."

"God help us Tucker, I can't believe I let you talk me into coming out here and having sex."

He chuckled. "Woman, sex is a natural thing between a woman and a man."

Laughing to herself, as she pulled her dress back on. "You'll say anything to get into my panties, Tucker."

He helped her zip up the back of her dress. "You know I will sweetheart."

Ada and Tucker laughed happily together as they climbed out of the RV.

A lone figure nestled against the shadows as he watched the two people head back to the hotel.

"Like mother, like daughter," Steele's thoughts said as he silently followed them.

Finding the RV had been easy. It was one of a kind.

Walking silently, at a safe distance, he thought of his life. He remembered back to the day he found out Colbert Granger was his real father. From the time he was a small boy he just knew Drake Coltrane, the man he called his father, wasn't his real father. But it was that day when he came home early from a friend's house that he overheard Drake and his mother arguing.

"You're nothing but Colbert's whore always was," Drake had yelled. "And the only reason why I stay with you is because Colbert Granger has paid me well for raising his bastard son!"

At that moment Steele hated the man named Drake Coltrane with a passion.

A few months later Steele watched earnestly as Drake choked on a roast beef sandwich.

Steele remembered vividly as beads of sweat rose on Drake's brow and his eyes budged wide.

Steele had felt nothing when Drake gasped for air, trying to call out for help.

Steele looked back into Drake's eyes with a look of utter surprise. In an instant he knew that Steele6 had heard what he called his mother that day. In an instant he knew it was the last thing he'd ever see again because he was dying.

Steele Coltrane had loved seeing his step-father dying just as he knew he'd love to see his real father and his half-brother pay for thinking he didn't matter.

He blended into the crowd as he watched Cierra's mother and her lover making their way to the elevator.

The crowded hotel lobby was filled with people on vacation, honeymooners, locals, gamblers and lovers enjoying themselves.

All at once, to Steele's surprise, Cierra and Ryker located her mother with her friend and mother and walked right up to them.

He felt a lump in his throat as his eyes gazed upon Cierra. He was a romantic fool since the moment he'd laid eyes on her the night of the charity event. Since that night she had consumed his mind as everything that was good.

He'd known dozens of beautiful women. But Cierra's beauty was mystical. She made him think thoughts of what his life would be like with a woman like Cierra. A woman who even his real father Colbert considered a good woman.

"Stay focused…Stay focused," he mumbled to himself as he hastily blended in with the crowded lobby of the casino. He found a slot machine within perfect view of where the small group was standing.

Steele hid well with a look of pure hatred on his face. He stared back at his half-brother Ryker, touching and fondling the woman that was supposed to have been his.

"Nobody takes the woman that was promised to me," he whispered to no one as the voices in his head screamed.

There was a laughter. Someone hit a jackpot on a slot machine several rows ahead of him. It shook Steele out of his thoughts.

He looked back to Cierra just in time to see her small party disperse. He watched as Cierra and her mother got on the elevator together.

Steele cleared his thoughts. He needed to get a room. But not here.

The Golden Palace Hotel was conveniently situated next door.

He made his exit.

Chapter 38

THE NEXT DAY.
"What kind a man gets dressed first thing in the morning and leaves his new wife alone to go down to the casino?" Cierra asked.

Ryker reached over and kissed her boldly. "A patient husband who knows he's got a firecracker in bed that could use a couple hours of sleep, alone."

He was content in knowing that Cierra enjoyed his sexual demands. It was the thing he loved about her most.

Cierra looked back at him with heavy dark eyes. "You really think I'm a firecracker?"

"Yes, a firecracker that needs some rest. You are so lucky I'm a lover who knows when to let his lady get some rest."

"Not to mention you are a lover who loves to ride. You rode me hard last night and half of this morning," she purred softly with a satisfied grin. "Not that a girl is complaining. I'm totally undeniably satisfied," she yawned.

"See my sweet firecracker. I'm right, you need rest. Besides, it's not first thing in the morning. It's almost four o'clock in the afternoon."

"Four o'clock," Cierra murmured. "Where does the time go? You're right Ryker. I could use a few hours of sleep. But first I want a hot bath."

"Whew, another chance to see you naked. I might not leave," he laughed, kissing her lips again.

"Hmmm, but a girl does need her alone time with her hot bath and some soap. I do need to get all cleaned up and fresh."

He licked the side of her neck. She tasted of sweat and sex. "I love the way that you taste. But I know you need that moment in a hot tub," he laughed and got up of off the bed.

He almost tripped over an empty bottle of champagne.

"Speaking of bottles, I'd love a bottle of water."

Ryker whistled while he finished dressing. "Tell you what I'll have room service bring by a salad and soup to go alone with the water."

"Perfect."

Ryker placed the order and made his exit.

***

Later Cierra laid relaxing in the luxuriating warm water. She found it strange to finally be all alone in the room. She laid her head back relaxing.

Suddenly she had an odd feeling she wasn't alone.

"Ma'am?" a female voice was saying. "Here's your bottled water. Would you like for me to open it for you?"

"Oh, yes," Cierra replied.

The woman handed her the opened bottled.

Cierra took a big gulp of the bottle water.

She turned to put a face to the female's voice. "This taste good," she said, taking another gulp.

The woman staring back at her had passive features, but her eyes was attentive.

"I'll let you get back to relaxing Ma'am,' the woman said. "I left you food on the table. Your husband already provided the tip," she said making her exit.

"Thank you," Cierra muttered, listening for the sound of the door closing.

At first Cierra thought she was dreaming as she felt the warmth of the bath engulf her. Then the voices in her head sounded loudly and vision faded in and out. She heard the ethereal music.

Suddenly she felt the bottle of water quivering in her hand. She blinked, trying to focus her eyes, then she dropped the bottle into the warm water as she felt her eyes grow heavy, and she lost consciousness.

She heard the voice say. "Come, get out of the water Cierra I will dry you off.

She opened one eye.

Her voice was raspy. "Ryker, you came back."

"Yes."

He pulled her naked body out of the tub and wrapped the towel around her. He then led her to the bed and laid her down.

His hands massaged her body vigorously with the towel.

"Hmmm," she moaned. "That feels so good," she said as his hands caressed and explored her body.

Their mouths made contact as she laid beneath, him feeling her legs spread wide as she felt his penis pushing, pushing further.

She groaned clinging to him.

The moment was mind blowing.

Chapter 39

"CIERRA? CIERRA PLEASE WAKE UP!"

"Mom! What is it?" Cierra said with a groggy moan.

"Here Cierra drink this."

"What is it?"

"Drink it. It's black coffee," Ada said.

Cierra finished the cup of black coffee and handed the empty cup back to her mother. She pushed back against the head board of the bed.

Ada put the empty cup down and wrung her hands together. She swallowed hard as she paced about.

Cierra stared curiously back at her mother, feeling something wasn't right.

"You little bitch!" Ada cried, as she slapped her across the face.

"Mom! What the hell is wrong with you?" Cierra screamed instinctively shielding her face. "What did I do?"

"What did you do?" Ada repeated rubbing her temple. "You have the gall to ask me that! Don't toy with me Cierra. I'm your mother."

Cierra searched her memory banks trying to remember. "Mom, I've been her sleeping all afternoon. I don't know what you're talking about. Why are you acting crazy?"

Ada studied Cierra's eyes. It took her a moment but then she guessed it. The man she saw leaving had a similar built as Ryker. In fact, at that moment the pieces of the puzzled began to fit. She fumed as her hands clasp her face.

Ada's thoughts raced as she rubbed her temple. "Of course! Of course, it all made sense. Why hadn't she seen it before? God he was using her baby Cierra as a pawn in his crazy game."

Ada swallowed hard trying to ignore the common-sense thought trying to fill her head. At that moment she didn't give a damn about doing the right thing. The only thing that matter to her was that her daughter was married and was going to stay married to Ryker Granger.

She rushed over to the bed.

"Cierra baby, Momma is so sorry. Please forgive me baby. We all need to get out of Las Vegas and get back home.

Epilogue

NINE MONTHS LATER, THE GRANGER
FAMILY home was filled with guests.

"Okay everyone, let me get a picture of Ryker and
Cierra surrounded by all their baby shower gifts," Isabella
yelled.

Ada walked up to the man who stood lonely off
away from the crowd. Her smile was taut. "I haven't seen
you around for ages."

"I've been busy," he said.

Ada's voice was flat as she placed the baby in his
arms. "My grandson is beautiful, isn't he?"

"Yes, he is."

"Come, let us talk in private," she said pulling him a
safe distance out of earshot.

Ada leaned in close and whispered. "My grandson
looks just like his father, aren't I right Steele?"

The angelic face of the sleeping baby stared back at
him.

At that moment Steele looked deep into her eyes
and scolded back at her with a deep look of contempt. He
got her meaning.

"Yes, I know what you did Steele. You gave my
daughter Cierra a drink that contained benzodiazepine and
then you raped her. Only you don't call it rape and well
Cierra can't remember."

"Oh really, and how do you know?"

"Don't worry about how I know. Just know that I know, and I have proof," she hesitated. I know that you were conveniently staying at the Golden Palace Hotel right next door to the hotel we all stayed at. When Cierra and Ryker were married. And that's not all I know. I know who supplied you with the benzodiazepine that night. And how you managed to get into their room."

The old woman was clever, Steele thought as he smiled back at her with a hideous mixture of triumph and loathing, until the baby stirred in his arms and his face went blank. He was standing there holding his baby and no one was approaching him. The old woman hadn't raised her voice one time.

"So, what is your reason for keeping this all a secret?"

Just at that moment Ada signaled for a young woman to come over. She took the baby from Steele's hands and handed it to the girl.

"Darlene, take the baby back over to Lana. I can tell she's anxious to hold him."

Once Darlene was out of earshot Ada turned to Steele. "Look how happy your father Colbert is watching Lana hold the baby. Think about it, Steele, Colbert has always been a part of your life even before he knew you were his son."

Steele looked back at her. "How did you know that?"

"Like I said before Steele, I'm a woman who does her homework. There's a lot of things about you that I made it a point to know.

Ada smiled knowingly. "Oh, by the way Steele you must meet my fiancé, "Tucker Justice Jones."

Steele looked up into the waiting eyes of Tucker Justice Jones. His mind was working swiftly and coolly.

"Hello Mr. Jones," Steele said swallowing. "I remember you."

Tucker Justice Jones had at one time been a special investigation agent for the San Jose Police Department, who was brought in for special circumstances cases. He was the agent who had questioned Steele after his step-father's death had been reported.

Tucker looked Steele in the eye. "Ada has one beautiful grandson. I'm sure we'll both be looking out for him, his mother and your brother Ryker. I'm sure we don't want any Takers trying to shatter that little families dreams of happiness."

Steele rubbed his chin and nodded murmuring under his breath. "I… I… I don't understand."

"Sure, you do Steele, just like I understood you when you confessed to me that you just stood there and watched your step-father choking to death. And instead of letting you get sucked into the juvenile correction system, I called your real father Colbert Granger and he made everything right for you.

Ada took Steele's hand and stared back into his face. "You see Tucker, I said Steele would understand. He doesn't have an evil look in his face."

"Yes, Ada darling, but you forget that there is an evil in some men's heart that does not show upon the face," Tucker replied.

With an effort Steele drew his hand away. Ada's grip was powerful. He stepped back a pace.

"Oh, by the way Steele," Ada said gently and coldly. "There is an old saying that he who plots evil will be known as a schemer," she said as her face filled with a determined expression.

All at once she burst into a cold crackle of laughter.

Steele looked curiously between Ada and Tucker as a momentary flash of fear flashed across his face.

Ada spoke slowly. "It is my opinion, Steele that death always comes to the schemer in the end. Like my wise dead grandmother was always fond of saying. When a taker dreams and he uses schemes to achieve his dreams, his dreams are best taken to his grave," she steadies her attentive gaze on Steel. "So, my daughter Cierra's secret is safe with you, right, Steele?"

Steele stared back in puzzled surprised at the amusement he saw staring back at him in Ada's eyes.

Slowly he nodded agreement.

Suddenly Tucker reached out and touched his arm.

He looked up sharply at Tucker and nodded he understood.

Tucker was shaking his head portentously. "You know what happens to evil people, don't you Steele. You've had a firsthand view before, right?"

"Ah, yes... I mean I understand completely. I think it's time for me to leave," Steele said and then he stopped abruptly and turned around. "Ms. Ada, could I ask you one question?"

Ada looked up at Tucker and he gave her a reassuring nod. She then turned to Steele and said. "Well, I guess so, what is it?"

"What color are my son's eyes?"

Awkwardly Ada blinked her eyes several times puzzled at the question. Slowly recognition registered. She started shaking her head and muttering. "Of course, why haven't I thought of that," she declared firmly. "Green! By grandson eyes are Granger Green!" She declared proudly.

Instantly Steele turn his back and hastily made his exit. He hurried to his SUV, got in and turned up the music loud. The sob escape from his throat. Fate had been cruel. Real cruel. "It's my fucking baby brother's son!"

The End

COMING

WINTER

2018

Book II
Mistress of Desire & The
Orchid Lover
~ The Quest
~ One Love In A
Lifetime!

COMING
SPRING
2019

DIAMONDS
At
Midnight

Books by J. A. Jackson

♥

A Geek an Angel Series
The Deceiver
The Proposition
The Grand Hotel
Lovers, Players, &
The Seducer Book I
Lovers, Players,
Revenge Book II

♥

The Mistress of Desire
& The Orchid Lover

♥

When A Taker Dreams

Lovers, Players & The Seducer
http://www.amazon.com/dp/B00MCEGUQA

The Mistress of Desire & The Orchid Lover
http://www.amazon.com/dp/B00ND6HV3C
The Grand Hotel
http://www.amazon.com/dp/B00CLF7JU6
The Deceiver
http://www.amazon.com/dp/B009Q6ICH2

The Proposition
http://www.amazon.com/dp/B00BE6EQT0

When a Taker Dreams

Cierra Cantrell has had little experience with men after a painful experience in her life left her too insecure to discover and free the passionate woman within.

http://www.amazon.com/dp/B01288VA7I

"When a Taker Dreams" is intensely steamy, sensual and suspenseful. If you're a Jackson fan you'll want to devour the entire novel all in one sitting, and if you've never read any Jackson novels before, you're in for a big treat!

 Don't miss out – get your copy now. Available on Amazon!

About the Author:

J.A. Jackson is the pseudonym for an author, who loves to write deliciously sultry adult novels that combine romance, suspense, and the unexpected, with an entertaining, unique twist.

Dear Gentle Readers

Dear Gentle Readers, Fans, Family and Friends,

Reviews for my books are what this author needs….
Let me explain.

In an effort to provide you with the most honest information about me. I confess I am a self-published author.

That's right, I am committed to writing a story, a novel every chance I get (hopefully I will put out two to three books a year). Even though I have a whacked-out, frenetic, hectic schedule as do many others. I persevere. I am committed to writing my stories.

With that said, I'd like to make a request of you my gentle readers, followers, friends, and family. I appreciate that you read my books. And I need you to please go to Amazon.com or KINDLE and review my book.

I will be truthful if you do. I would like for you to help me.

Your kindness to me in reviewing my books would go a long way in helping me continue my self-publishing journey.

Thank you for all that you do. I truly appreciate you!
Sincerely,
J. A. Jackson
Email: jerreecejackson@gmail.com

Questions I have been asked!

What does my fans mean to me?
 Point blank period they are the wind beneath my feet.
Their enthusiasm and support for my books are most
graciously appreciated my me. Not only that their support
enables me to continue with my writing. In fact, because of
several fans, who learned that I grew up in Chicago,
encourage me to write about a book with it taking place in
Chicago.   So, to summarize, I truly appreciate and am
grateful for my fans. Their support means everything to me.

What are you currently working on?
I am currently working on Book III of Lovers' Players and
The Seducer. I haven't really set the title in stone yet. But
it is along the lines of the Prodigal Son returning home.
In addition, I have completed a book I call, Diamond at
Midnight. This story takes place in Chicago. I have the
book jacket and editing completed. I just need to give it a
final read through and then make it available for "Pre-sale".

As of November 3, 2018, I will be releasing Book II of
Mistress of Desire and the Orchid Lover.

Where do you get your ideas?
My ideas come from being inspired by the fabulous
grandiose landscape of the magnificent State of California.
For example, for the Grand Hotel my inspiration came from
walking past the royal old Sir Drake Hotel on Powell Street
in San Francisco one night and the rest was a novel.

Do you ever experience writer's block, if so, how do you deal with it?
 From time to time I experience writers block and normally
when I do it means I need to get out of the house and get
away from my normal routine. When this normally happens
my husband and I go for long car rides. We visit faraway

places (in California).   We especially love visiting small towns and taking drives on the coast. I find it always frees up the "what if" moments in my mind.

What advice would you offer to aspiring writers? Persevere! Then never stop believing in yourself. Next, I would say always listen to the voice within. It is your number one fan and keep pushing yourself to completion of your novel. Because you really are more capable than you know. Believe in yourself.   And finally, I would say remember NO is not fatal. Ignore the folks who say no because somebody will say yes.
Got a question for Author J. A. Jackson? Email me at jerreecejackson@yahoo.com

Discover all the deliciously Romantic, Suspenseful, and Entertaining Novels by author J. A. Jackson, each with unique surprises and something for every reader here!

https://www.amazon.com/author/jajackson

<u>Thank you</u> for all that you do. I truly appreciate you!